Bedtime Stories

for Boys

Illustrated by
Jeremy Bays, Natalie Bould, Lynn Breeze, Anna Cattermole,
Maureen Galvani, Mary Hall, Virginia Margerison, Paula Martyr,
Julia Oliver, Martin Orme, Sara Silcock, Gillian Toft, Charlie Ann Turner,
Kerry Vaughan, Jenny Williams and Kirsty Wilson

This is a Parragon Book
This edition published in 2002

Parragon
Queen Street House
4 Queen Street
Bath BA1 1HE, UK

Printed and bound in Dubai
ISBN 0-75259-553-9

Bedtime Stories
for Boys

Written by Derek Hall, Alison Morris and Louisa Somerville

Contents

Granny Casts a Spell

Susie was very fond of her Granny. Each day, when Susie got home from school, Granny was always there sitting by the fire knitting. Granny knitted so fast that sometimes it seemed as though the knitting needles sparked in the firelight.

"Do you know," Granny would say, "that I'm really a witch?" Susie always laughed when Granny said that because she didn't look at all like a witch. She had a smiling face and kind eyes and she never wore black. Not ever. When Granny wasn't looking, Susie would take a peek inside her wardrobe just in case she might find a broomstick or a witch's hat. But she never found so much as a book of spells.

"I don't believe you're a witch," said Susie.

"I am," replied Granny, "and I'll cast a spell one day. You'll know when that day comes, for my needles will start to knit by themselves." After that, Susie kept a careful watch over Granny's needles, but they always lay quite still in the basket of knitting.

One day, Susie was playing in her garden when she heard the sound of weeping. The sound seemed to be coming from under the old tree in the corner. She walked towards the tree and as she did so the crying noise got louder, but she could not see anyone there. Then she looked down at her feet and there – sitting on a mossy stone – was a tiny little man. He was neatly dressed in a yellow velvet waistcoat and knickerbockers. On his feet were beautiful, shiny, buckled shoes, and a three-cornered hat with a wren's feather in it trembled on his shaking head. When the little man saw Susie, he stopped crying and started to dab his eyes with a fine lace handkerchief.

"Whatever can the matter be?" asked Susie, crouching down.

"Oh dear, oh dear!" sobbed the little man, "I am the fairy princess's tailor and she has asked me to make her a lovely gown to wear to the May Ball tonight, but a wicked elf has played a

trick on me and turned all my fine gossamer fabric into bats'
wings. Now I shall never be able to make the princess's gown and
she will be very angry with me." He started to cry again.

"Don't cry!" said Susie. "I'm sure I can help. My Granny's got
a sewing basket full of odds and ends. I'll see if she's got anything
nice for a party dress. I'm sure she won't mind sparing some –
after all, you won't need much," she said. At that, the little man
looked a bit more cheerful.

"Wait here," said Susie, "while I run indoors and see." She ran
up the garden path and in through the back door.

"Granny, Granny!" she called. She ran into the sitting room
expecting to find Granny knitting by the fire. But Granny had her
eyes closed and she was whispering to herself. On her lap was her
knitting – and the needles were moving all by themselves, so that the
yarn danced up and down on the old lady's knees.

8

For a moment, Susie was too astounded to move. Then she thought, "I hope Granny's not casting a bad spell. I'd better make sure the little tailor is alright."

She ran back down the garden path and there under the tree sat the tailor, surrounded by a great pile of gorgeous gossamer, shining in the sunlight.

"I've never seen such fine material – ever!" he exclaimed. "But where did it come from? I just closed my eyes to dab them with my hanky and when I opened them again – there it was!"

"I don't know," said Susie, "but I think my Granny might have had something to do with it."

"Well, I'd never be able to thank her enough," said the tailor. "For now I shall be able to make the finest gown in the whole of fairyland. The princess will dance the night away in the prettiest dress there ever was." He paused and then went on, "I'm also indebted to you, for it was you who helped me in the first place. I would like it very much if you came to the May Ball, too."

"Why, thank you so much," Susie replied, "I should like that very much." She didn't want to hurt the tailor's feelings but she knew she couldn't go – she was far too big to go to a fairy ball!

"Well I must get on with the dress now," said the little man, reaching for a pair of fairy scissors. "See you tonight!" And with that he vanished.

Susie went indoors again. Granny was knitting by the fire as usual. Susie wondered if she had dreamed the whole thing. Everything seemed so normal. Really, how could she have imagined she'd seen a fairy tailor in the garden! And as for Granny casting a spell!

That night, Susie lay in bed and wondered if the fairies really were having a ball. How she longed to be there! Once she thought she heard a tapping at the window. Was that the fairy tailor she saw through the glass – or was she imagining it? In the middle of the night she awoke with a start. There was a click, clicking noise at the end of her bed.

10

"Granny is that you?" called Susie.

"Yes, dear," replied Granny. "I couldn't sleep, so I decided to do some knitting. All at once the needles started twitching, so I knew it was time to cast a spell. What is your wish, Susie?"

"I... I...," stammered Susie, "I want to go to the May Ball," she blurted.

"Then you shall, my dear," said Granny.

In an instant, Susie felt herself shrinking and when she looked down she saw she was wearing a beautiful gown and tiny satin slippers. Then she floated on gossamer wings out through the window and off to the Ball.

The next morning, Susie woke up in her bed. Had it all been a dream – the revelry, the fairy food, the frog band, the dance with the fairy prince? Then she saw something peeping out from under her pillow. And what do you think it was? It was a tiny, tiny shred of the finest gossamer fabric.

The Ugly Duckling

Once upon a time, there was a mother duck who laid a clutch of six beautiful little eggs. One day, she looked into her nest in amazement. For there were her six small eggs but lying next to them was another egg that was much, much bigger than the others. "That's odd," she thought, and went back to sitting on the nest.

Soon, one by one, the smaller eggs hatched, and out came six pretty yellow ducklings. Yet the bigger egg still had not hatched.

The mother duck sat on the large egg for another day and another night until eventually the egg cracked, and out tumbled a seventh duckling.

But this one was very different. He was big, with scruffy grey feathers and large brown feet.

"You do look different from my other chicks," exclaimed the mother duck, "but never mind, I'm sure you've got a heart of gold." And she cuddled him to her with all the other ducklings. Sure enough, he was very sweet-natured and happily played alongside the other ducklings.

One day, the mother duck led her ducklings down to the river to learn to swim. One by one they jumped into the water and splashed about. But when the big grey duckling leaped into the water he swam beautifully. He could swim faster and further than any of his brothers or sisters. The other ducklings were jealous and began to resent him.

"You're a big ugly duckling," they hissed at him. "You don't belong here." And when their mother wasn't looking they chased him right away.

The ugly duckling felt very sad as he waddled away across the fields. "I know I'm not fluffy and golden like my brothers and sisters," he said to himself. "I may have scruffy grey feathers and big brown feet, but I'm just as good as they are – and I'm

14

better at swimming!" He sat down under a bush and started to cry. Just then he heard a terrible sound – CRACK! CRACK! It was the sound of a gun. There were men out there shooting ducks. Then, only a short way from where he was hiding, a dog rushed past him, sniffing the ground. The ugly duckling did not dare to move. He stayed under the bush until it was dark and only then did he feel it was safe to come out.

He set off, not knowing which way he was going until eventually, through the darkness, he saw a light shining. The light came from a cosy-looking cottage. The ugly duckling looked inside cautiously. He could see a fire burning in the hearth and sitting by the fire was an old woman with a hen and a cat.

"Come in, little duckling," said the old woman. "You are welcome to stay here. For now I can have duck's eggs each day as well as hen's eggs."

The ugly duckling was glad to warm himself by the fire. When the old lady had gone to bed, the hen and the cat cornered the duckling.

"Can you lay eggs?" enquired the hen.

"No," replied the duckling.

"Can you catch mice?" demanded the cat.

"No," replied the miserable duckling.

"Well, you're no use then, are you?" they sneered.

The next day, the old woman scolded the duckling: "You've been here a whole day and not one egg! You're no use, are you?"

So the ugly duckling waddled off out of the cottage. "I know when I'm not wanted," he said to himself mournfully.

He wandered along for a very long time until at last he reached a lake where he could live without anyone to bother him. He lived on the lake for many months. Gradually the days got shorter and the nights longer. The wind blew the leaves off the trees. Winter came and the weather turned bitterly cold. The lake froze over and the ugly duckling shivered under the reeds at the lake's edge. He was desperately cold, hungry and lonely, but he had nowhere else to go.

At last spring came, the weather got warmer and the ice on the lake melted. The ugly duckling felt the sun on his feathers. "I think I'll go for a swim," he thought. He swam right out into the middle of the lake, where the water was as clear as a mirror. He looked down at his reflection in the water and stared and stared. Staring back at him was a beautiful white bird with a long, elegant neck. "I'm no longer an ugly duckling," he said to himself, "but what am I?"

At that moment three big white birds just like himself flew towards him and landed on the lake. They swam right up to him and one of them said, "You are the handsomest swan that we have ever seen. Would you care to join us?"

"So *that's* what I am – I'm a swan," thought the bird that had been an ugly duckling. "I would love to join you," he said to the other swans. "Am I really a swan?" he asked, not quite believing it could be true.

"Of course you are!" replied the others. "Can't you see you're just like us?"

The three older swans became his best friends and the ugly duckling, that was now a beautiful swan, swam across the lake with them and there they lived together. He knew that he was one of them and that he would never be lonely again.

Catswhiskers

Catswhiskers was a pyjama case cat, and a very fine-looking pyjama case cat at that. Susie's granny had sewn him together when Susie was only four years old. It had taken Susie's granny quite a long time to make Catswhiskers. Every night she had sat by the fire carefully cutting and sewing, until he was perfect. Catswhiskers' body was made from the finest black velvet. He had beautiful red glass eyes, a bushy tail and the longest whiskers you have ever seen. That is how he got the name Catswhiskers. Catswhiskers sat on the end of Susie's bed, looking at all the toys in the bedroom in that slightly snooty way that cats have of looking at things.

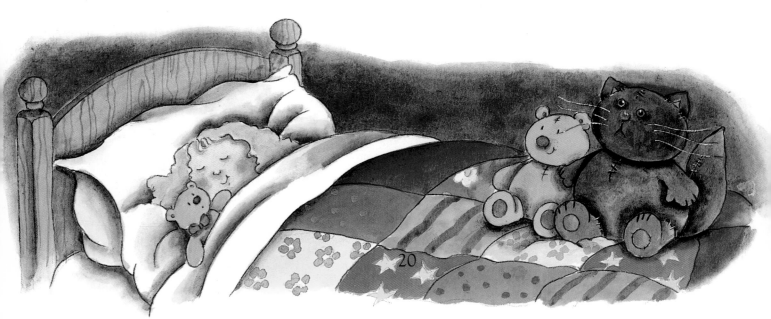

20

When Susie was asleep, or playing in another room, Catswhiskers and all the toys would talk to each other. But Catswhiskers was bored with talking to the toys. Jenny the ragdoll was – well – just a ragdoll. "What could a ragdoll possibly have to say that would be of interest to a velvet pyjama case cat?" thought Catswhiskers.

Then there was Neddy the rocking horse. He was a perfectly pleasant rocking horse as far as rocking horses went, but he only ever seemed to want to talk about how nice and shiny he was, and how he thought he was Susie's favourite toy. Even the alphabet bricks, the jack-in-the-box and the brightly coloured ball seemed to have nothing to say of interest to Catswhiskers. He sighed and looked at the window, wondering if life was more exciting outside.

21

One day, he decided he'd had enough of life in the bedroom with all the toys, and that he would venture outside to see if he could meet someone more interesting to talk to. So that night, when it was dark and Susie was asleep, he crept carefully to the open bedroom window and jumped out. It was a clear, cold, moonlit night. Catswhiskers shivered a little to find it so cold outside, and he maybe shivered a little more because he was also rather frightened. But he was very excited to be in the outside world, too, and he soon forgot about the cold and his fear.

He walked along the fence to the end of Susie's garden and jumped down into the garden next door. He had no sooner landed when he heard a fierce growl and saw two big, black eyes glinting in the moonlight.

It was Barker, next door's dog – and he didn't like cats at all. With a loud bark, Barker came rushing towards Catswhiskers. His mouth was open wide and Catswhiskers could see his big, sharp teeth. In fact, he thought that he could see all the way down into Barker's stomach! Catswhiskers only just had time to leap back on to the fence as Barker, jaws still snapping, gave chase.

"Phew, what a narrow escape," gasped Catswhiskers. "I didn't realise dogs were so unfriendly!"

He was wondering where it might be safe to go next when he heard a low, hissing voice behind him. "Hey, velvet cat," hissed the voice. "What do you think you are doing on *our* patch?"

Catswhiskers turned round to see the biggest, meanest-looking cat he had ever set eyes on. And behind *him* were several more mean-looking cats, all coming slowly towards Catswhiskers with their sharp claws at the ready. Catswhiskers didn't wait a second longer. He simply ran for his life.

Now he was very frightened. He was also feeling cold and hungry. He wished that he was still in the warm safety of Susie's bedroom with the other toys. Just as he was thinking that the outside world was perhaps a bit *too* exciting, he heard the sound of a van approaching. It suddenly stopped, its glaring headlights shining straight at him. On the side of the van were the words STRAY CAT CATCHER.

Out of the van stepped a man carrying a big net. Catswhiskers thought he knew just who that net was for, and decided that it was definitely time to go!

Without thinking about the dangers he might find himself in if he came face to face again with gangs of sharp-clawed cats or fierce, barking dogs, he ran back towards Susie's house as fast as his velvet legs could carry him. At last he reached the window and jumped thankfully back inside.

Snuggled down again on the warm bed with all his familiar friends around him, Catswhiskers decided that perhaps this was the best life for a pyjama case cat after all.

The King Who Ate Too Much

Long ago, in a kingdom far, far away, there lived a greedy king. Now the thing that this king loved, more than anything else in the whole world, was food. He simply couldn't get enough of it. Ever since he was a little prince, he had been allowed to eat whatever he wanted, whenever he wanted it. And because he was always eating, he just got fatter and fatter and fatter with every day that passed.

When he became king, his appetite seemed to get even bigger! As soon as he woke in the morning, he would have his servants bring him an enormous breakfast. After eating several huge, steaming bowls of porridge, he would eat slice after slice of hot, buttered toast and jam, followed by all the boiled eggs that the royal chickens could lay.

In case he got a little hungry mid-morning, he would have a snack – usually ten or more chocolate cakes, washed down with as many cups of tea!

At lunchtime, the table would groan with the weight of all the pies, sandwiches, fruit and biscuits that the greedy king was about to gobble down.

For afternoon tea, it would be cakes, cakes and more cakes.

But the king's biggest meal was supper! The royal cooks toiled for most of the day to prepare this feast. When it was time for the king to eat, one servant after another would carry in great bowls of steaming soup, plates of fish of every kind, followed by huge roasts and dishes of vegetables. Down it all went, followed by fruit and jelly. At last, the king would be full and he would retire to his bed for the night.

But the king's greedy eating habits also made him a very thoughtless king. No-one dared tell him that much of the wealth of the kingdom had to be spent on his huge meals. In the meantime, his loyal subjects were going hungry and becoming poor and needy.

One day, just after the king had eaten his usual big lunch, he began to feel very strange. Not only did he feel even bigger than usual, he also began to feel very light. Suddenly, without any warning, he started floating up from the table and into the air like a big balloon.

"Help! Get me down!" he cried.

28

The royal courtiers and servants jumped up and down and tried in vain to grab the king as he floated upwards, but in no time at all he had floated out of reach. Before anyone knew it, he had floated out of the castle window. Out across the royal grounds he went, over the river and towards the woods and mountains of his kingdom.

"Wooaa-aaah!" cried the king, as he disappeared from view.

Soon, the king began to float over a small farm. He looked down and saw the farmer's children, dressed only in rags, searching for firewood. Some thin, hungry cows stood nearby chewing on a few meagre pieces of hay.

Over the next farm he floated, and a similar sad scene met his gaze. Dressed in rags, a poor farmer and his family toiled their soil hoping to grow enough to eat.

Next he floated over a small village. Everywhere he looked he saw shabby, run-down houses in need of repair and people in the streets begging for money.

Every farm and every village the king floated over told the same story of hunger and misery. The king suddenly felt very sad and very ashamed. He had been so busy enjoying himself eating that he hadn't given a thought to the plight of his subjects. While he was getting fatter and fatter, they were all getting thinner and poorer.

Now, a gust of wind was blowing the king back towards his castle. As he was passing over the castle, he suddenly felt himself falling. Down, down, he went until he landed back into the castle grounds with a great thud and a bounce.

That very day, the king sent out a royal proclamation. All his loyal subjects were to come to the castle for a huge feast, after which they would all be given a purse full of gold.

As for the king, he was never greedy again. Instead of spending all his money on food for himself, he gave enough to all the people in the land so that they would never be hungry or poor again.

31

The Singing Bear

Long ago, there lived a young boy named Peter. He was a gentle lad who loved all creatures, but most of all he loved the animals and birds of the forest. Many a time he had mended a jay's broken wing, or set a badger free from a cruel trap.

One day, the fair came to town and Peter was very excited. He could see brightly coloured tents being put up in the field and carts arriving with mysterious looking loads. As soon as the fair was open Peter was off with his penny in his pocket to try his luck. First of all he had a go at the coconut shy. Then he tried to climb the greasy pole. Finally, he used his last farthing on the tombola stall. He was about to head for home when out of the corner of his eye he caught a glimpse of a dreadful sight. Lying in a cage, looking sad and forlorn, was a large brown bear. On a small plate at the front of the cage was the bear's name: Lombard. He looked so dejected that Peter immediately vowed to set him free. The cage was strongly padlocked and Peter knew not how he could break the lock. He turned to make his way home, with the bear gazing pitifully after him.

That night, Peter tossed and turned in his bed. What was he to do? He wasn't strong enough to break into the bear's cage and his keeper would surely not agree to set him free. In the middle of the night, he resolved to return to the fairground to comfort the bear.

He slipped out of bed and made his way by the light of the moon back to the fairground. To his astonishment he found the bear singing a song to himself in a beautiful voice. For a while Peter listened to the lovely sound of the bear's singing. Then he had an idea. He remembered a piece of paper he had seen pinned to the palace gate.

33

"Don't cry, Lombard," he said. "I think I know a way to get you out of here. But first you must teach me your song." The bear was happy to oblige and soon the two of them were singing the song together. Then Peter said, "I must go, but I'll be back tomorrow. And remember, when you see me, be ready to sing your song."

The next day, Peter put on his very best clothes and set off for the palace. Pinned to the gate was the piece of paper, just as Peter had remembered. On the paper was written in a handsome script: *The King Requires a Minstrel with a Fine Voice. Apply Within.*

Peter knocked at the gate. He was shown into a beautiful golden gallery where a row of minstrels were waiting to be auditioned. A courtier rang a little bell for silence, and in came the king. He sat down at his great gold throne.

"Let the audition begin," cried the king. The first minstrel stepped forward. He sang a song in a sweet, high voice that tugged at the heart and reduced the court to tears. The next minstrel sang in a deep, rich voice that sent shivers down the spine, so that the birds in the trees stopped singing to listen. The next minstrel sang a song that was so witty and amusing that the entire court wept with laughter.

At last it was Peter's turn. He stepped forward, gave a deep

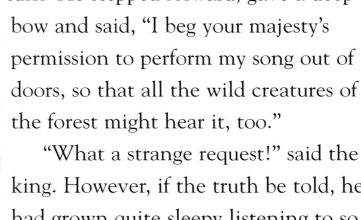

bow and said, "I beg your majesty's permission to perform my song out of doors, so that all the wild creatures of the forest might hear it, too."

"What a strange request!" said the king. However, if the truth be told, he had grown quite sleepy listening to so many beautiful songs and thought the fresh air might liven him up. "Very well, but it had better be worth it!" he said, giving Peter a fierce look.

"Follow me!" called Peter. He led the king, the court and all the minstrels out of the palace gates and down the road.

"Where are we going?" and "This is very untoward," they muttered. At last they reached the fairground, but Peter didn't stop until he was in view of Lombard's cage. Lombard saw him and Peter winked at the bear.

"This is where I'd like to sing for you," said Peter to the king.

The king's royal eyebrows rose higher and higher as he looked around him. "Well, I must say this is very odd indeed! However, as we've come this far, we may as well hear your song. Proceed!" said the king.

Peter opened his mouth and mimed the words while Lombard sang. It was the most beautiful song that anyone had ever heard. By the end of the song, the king was sobbing tears of joy, mirth and sorrow all together.

"That was the finest song I ever heard," he said. "You have won the audition and I would like you to be my minstrel."

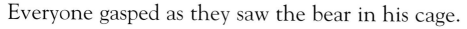

Peter took another low bow. "Sire," he said. "Would that I could accept, but in all honesty it was not I who sang but my friend, Lombard the bear." Everyone gasped as they saw the bear in his cage.

For a moment the king looked furious. But then he began to smile and said, "I praise you for your honesty, Peter, and I would very much like to have Lombard for my minstrel. Chancellor, bring me the royal purse."

The king paid Lombard's keeper handsomely, who was then delighted to set the bear free. Lombard became the king's minstrel and was famous throughout the land, and from then on Peter went to the palace each day and sang duets with his friend, the bear. And it is said that, in the end, Peter married the king's daughter.

37

The Greedy Hamster

There was once a hamster named Harry. He was a very greedy hamster. As soon as his food was put in his cage he gobbled it all up, and then he would push his little nose through the bars in the hope that something else to eat might come within reach. From his cage he could see all manner of delicious food on the kitchen table – and the smells! The scent of freshly baked bread was enough to send him spinning round in his exercise wheel with frustration.

"It's not fair!" he grumbled to himself. "They're all eating themselves silly out there and here am I simply starving to death!" (At this point he would usually remember the large meal he had just eaten and that his tummy was indeed still rather full.)

"If only I could get out of this beastly cage, I could feast on all the food I deserve," he announced to himself, and the thought of all those tasty morsels made his mouth water.

One night after the family had gone to bed, Harry was having one last spin in his wheel before retiring to his sawdust mattress. As he spun around, he heard an unfamiliar squeaky noise.

"That's funny," thought Harry. "The little girl oiled my wheel only today. It surely can't need oiling again." He stopped running and got off the wheel, but the squeak continued. Harry sat quite still on his haunches and listened intently. Then he realised it was the door to his cage squeaking. The door! The door was flapping open. The little girl had not closed it properly before she went to bed. Harry did a little dance of glee. Then he went to the door and looked cautiously out in case there was any danger. But all seemed to be well. The cat was asleep on a chair. The dog was sleeping soundly on the floor.

Now, as well as being a greedy hamster, Harry was also clever. Once outside the cage, the first thing he did was look at the catch to see how it worked. Yes! He was pretty sure he could work out how to open it from the inside now. Harry sniffed the air. There were some tasty titbits left over from a birthday party on the table. He could smell the sugar icing, and soon he was on the table, cramming his mouth with odds and ends of cheese sandwiches and pieces of chocolate cake. When he had eaten his fill, he stuffed his cheek pouches with ginger biscuits and ran back into his cage, closing the door behind him.

"Good!" thought Harry. "Now I will never be hungry again."

The next night Harry let himself out of his cage and helped himself to food, and again the next night and the night after that. He feasted on everything and anything – nuts, bananas, pieces of bread, left-over jelly and slices of pizza were all pushed into his greedy mouth. Each time he returned to his cage he filled his cheeks with more and more food. He did not notice that he was getting fatter and fatter, although he was aware that he could no longer run round in his wheel without falling off! Then one night, he undid the door catch but found he was simply too wide to get through the door!

For a while Harry sat in a very bad temper in the corner of the cage. His cheeks were still bulging with food from his last midnight feast, but the greedy hamster wanted more. Then he had an idea. "I'll get that lazy cat to help," he thought. He squealed at the top of his voice until the cat, who had been dreaming of rats, woke up with a start.

"What do you want?" she hissed at Harry. Harry explained his problem.

41

"Of course, I'd be only too pleased to help," said the crafty cat, thinking to herself here was an extra dinner! With her strong claws she bent back the door frame of the cage, until there was just enough room for Harry to squeeze through. Then, with a mighty swipe of her paw, she caught him and gobbled him whole. She felt extremely full, what with Harry and all his food inside her. She could barely crawl back to her chair and soon she was fast asleep again and snoring loudly with her mouth open. Inside her tummy Harry, too, felt very uncomfortable. Every time the cat snored, it sounded like a thunderstorm raging around his head.

"I must get out of here," he thought, and headed for the cat's open jaws. But he was far too fat to get out again. Then he had another idea. Through the cat's jaws he could see the dog lying on the floor.

"Help! Help!" he squeaked. The dog woke up to a very strange sight. There was the cat lying on the chair snoring, but she also seemed to be squeaking, "Help!" The dog put his head on one side. He was very perplexed. Then he saw a pair of beady eyes and some fine whiskers inside the cat's mouth. It was Harry!

"Get me out of here, please," pleaded Harry.

Now the dog did not very much like the cat, so he was quite willing to help the hamster.

"I'll stick my tail in the cat's mouth. Then you hang on while I pull you out," said the dog. "But mind you don't make a sound and wake the cat, or she'll surely bite my tail!" The dog gingerly put the tip of his tail inside the cat's open jaws, just far enough for Harry's little paws to grab hold. Then he pulled with all his might. Out popped Harry and out of Harry popped all the food he'd stored in his cheeks – peanuts, an apple core and a slice of jam tart!

"Thank you, thank you," gasped Harry as he made a dash for his cage and slammed the door shut. "I think I'll stay in my cage from now on and just stick to the food I'm given!"

The Mean King and the Crafty Lad

There was once a king who was as mean as he was rich. He lived in a great palace where he spent his days counting his bags of gold coins. Meanwhile his subjects lived in great poverty. Sometimes the king would summon his page to prepare the royal carriage. Then the king would set forth in his great, golden coach to survey his kingdom.

Now not only was the king extremely rich, but he was very vain. As he passed his subjects working in the field, he liked them to bow to him and pay him compliments. "How handsome you look today, your majesty!" they would call, or "How well the colour pink suits you, Sire!"

His head would swell with pride as he moved on. "My people truly adore me!" he would say.

But for all their complimentary words, the people hated their king. They resented the fact that the king lived in splendour while his subjects toiled hard all their lives. At last a secret meeting was called among the peasants. "Let's sign a petition demanding our rights!" cried one man.

"And fair pay!" shouted another. They all cheered and clapped their hands.

"Who's going to write down our demands?" called an old woman. Now the crowd was hushed, for none of them knew how to read or write.

"I know what we can do instead," called a voice from the back. Everyone turned round to see a young lad in rags. "Let's march on the palace!" he cried.

"Yes!" roared the crowd.

As the angry mob reached the palace, the king saw them and sent out his guard dogs. The peasants were forced to flee for their lives with the dogs snapping at their ankles. Not until the last peasant was out of sight did the king call off his dogs.

"Good work!" he cried.

From then on, however, life became even harder for the people because the king was on his guard in case they marched on the castle again. Now, when he went out and about in his kingdom, he was always accompanied by his hounds.

Eventually, another secret meeting was called. "What can we do?" the people said. "We will never be able to get past those savage dogs."

"I've got an idea," came a familiar voice. It was the ragged lad again. For a while there was uproar as folk accused him of having nearly lost them their lives. "Please trust me," pleaded the lad. "I know I let you down, but this time I've got a well thought-out plan to get the king to give up his money." In the end, the peasants listened to the boy's scheme and decided to let him try.

The next day, the boy hid in a branch of a tree that overhung the palace garden. With him he had some dog biscuits, in which he had hidden a powerful sleeping pill. He threw the biscuits on to the palace lawn and waited. Some time later, as the boy had hoped, the king's hounds came out on to the lawn. They headed straight for the biscuits and gobbled them up. Soon they were fast asleep, one and all.

Quickly the lad slid out of the tree and, donning a large black cape, he ran round to the front of the palace and rapped on the door. A sentry opened the door. "Good day," said the lad, "I am Victor, the world-famous vet. Do you have any animals requiring medical attention?"

"No," replied the sentry, slamming the door in the lad's face. Just then voices could be heard from within the palace. After a few moments, the sentry opened the door again and said, "As a matter of fact, we do have a bit of a problem. Step inside."

The sentry led the lad out to the lawn where the king was weeping over the dogs' bodies. "Oh, please help," he cried. "I need my dogs. Without them I may be besieged by my own people."

47

The lad pretended to examine the dogs. He said to the king, "I have only seen one case like this before. The only cure is to feed the animals liquid gold."

"Liquid gold?" exclaimed the king. "Wherever shall I find liquid gold?"

"Fear not," said the lad, "I have a friend – a witch – who lives in the mountains. She can turn gold coins into liquid gold. You must let me take the dogs – and a bag of gold – to her and she will cure them."

Well, the king was so beside himself with fear that he readily agreed. The sleeping dogs were loaded on to a horse-drawn cart, and the king gave the lad a bag of gold saying, "Hurry back, my dogs are most precious."

Off went the lad, back to his home. His mother and father helped him unload the dogs, who by now were beginning to wake up. They took great care of the dogs, who were glad to be looked after kindly for once. The next day the lad put on the

48

cloak again and returned to the palace. "The good news is," he said to the king, "that the cure is working. The bad news is that there was only enough gold to revive one dog. I'll need all the gold you've got to cure the others."

"Take it all," screamed the king, "only I must have my dogs back tomorrow!" He opened the safe and threw his entire stock of gold on to another cart, which the young lad dragged away.

That night the lad gave each of the king's subjects a bag of gold. The next morning he led the dogs back to the palace. To his surprise, the king didn't want them back. "Now I have no gold," he said, "I don't need guard dogs."

Then the lad saw that the king had learned his lesson, and he told the king what had really happened. And to everyone's joy, the king said the peasants could keep their bags of gold. As for the king, he kept the dogs as pets and became a much nicer person.

The Boy Who Wished Too Much

There once was a young boy named Billy. He was a lucky lad, for he had parents who loved him, plenty of friends and a room full of toys. Behind his house was a rubbish tip. Billy had been forbidden to go there by his mother, but he used to stare at it out of the window. It looked such an exciting place to explore.

One day, Billy was staring at the rubbish tip, when he saw something gold-coloured gleaming in the sunlight. There, on the top of the tip, sat a brass lamp. Now Billy knew the tale of Aladdin, and he wondered if this lamp could possibly be magic, too. When his mother wasn't looking he slipped out of the back door, scrambled up the tip and snatched the lamp from the top.

Billy ran to the garden shed. It was quite dark inside, but Billy could see the brass of the lamp glowing softly in his hands. When his eyes had grown accustomed to the dark, he saw that the lamp was quite dirty. As he started to rub at the brass, there was a puff of smoke and the shed was filled with light. Billy closed his eyes tightly and when he opened them again, he found to his astonishment that there was a man standing there, dressed in a costume richly embroidered with gold and jewels. "I am the genie of the lamp," he said. "Are you by any chance Aladdin?"

"N… n… no, I'm Billy," stammered Billy, staring in disbelief.

"How very confusing," said the genie frowning. "I was told that the boy with the lamp was named Aladdin. Oh well, never mind! Now I'm here, I may as well grant you your wishes. You can have three, by the way."

At first Billy was so astonished he couldn't speak. Then he began to think hard. What would be the very best thing to wish for? He had an idea. "My first wish," he said, "is that I can have as many wishes as I want."

51

The genie looked rather taken aback, but then he smiled and said, "A wish is a wish. So be it!"

Billy could hardly believe his ears. Was he really going to get all his wishes granted? He decided to start with a really big wish, just in case the genie changed his mind later. "I wish I could have a purse that never runs out of money," he said.

Hey presto! There in his hand was a purse with five coins in it. Without remembering to thank the genie, Billy ran out of the shed and down the road to the sweet shop.

He bought a large bag of sweets and took one of the coins out of his purse to pay for it. Then he peeped cautiously inside the purse, and sure enough there were still five coins. The magic had worked! Billy ran back to the garden shed to get his next wish, but the genie had vanished. "That's not fair!" cried Billy, stamping his foot. Then he remembered the lamp. He seized it and rubbed at it furiously. Sure enough, the genie reappeared.

"Don't forget to share those sweets with your friends," he said.

"What is your wish, Billy?"

This time Billy, who was very fond of sweet things, said, "I wish I had a house made of chocolate!"

No sooner had he uttered the words than he found that he was standing outside a house made entirely of rich, creamy chocolate. Billy broke off the door knocker and nibbled at it. Yes, it really was made of the most delicious chocolate that he had ever tasted! Billy gorged himself until he began to feel quite sick. He lay down on the grass and closed his eyes. When he opened them again, the chocolate house had vanished and he was outside the garden shed once more. "It's not fair to take my chocolate house away. I want it back!" he complained, stamping his foot once again.

Billy went back into the shed. "This time I'll ask for something that lasts longer," he thought. He rubbed the lamp and there stood the genie again.

"You've got chocolate all around your mouth," said the genie disapprovingly. "What is your wish?"

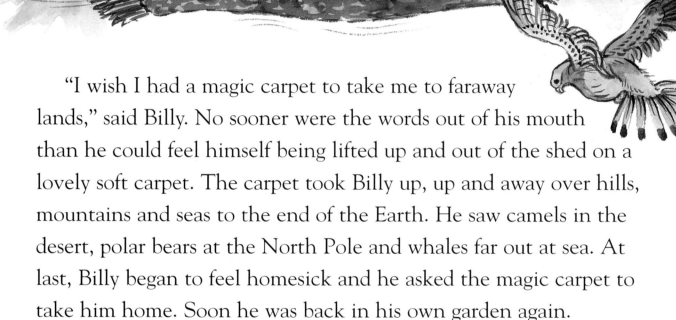

"I wish I had a magic carpet to take me to faraway lands," said Billy. No sooner were the words out of his mouth than he could feel himself being lifted up and out of the shed on a lovely soft carpet. The carpet took Billy up, up and away over hills, mountains and seas to the end of the Earth. He saw camels in the desert, polar bears at the North Pole and whales far out at sea. At last, Billy began to feel homesick and he asked the magic carpet to take him home. Soon he was back in his own garden again.

Billy was beginning to feel very powerful and important. He began to wish for more and more things. He wished that he did not have to go to school – and so he didn't! He wished that he had a servant to clear up after him and a cook to make him special meals of sweet things – and a cook and a servant appeared.of sweet things – and a cook and a servant appeared.

Billy began to get very fat and lazy. His parents despaired at how spoiled he had become. His friends no longer came to play because he had grown so boastful.

One morning, Billy woke up, looked in the mirror and burst into tears. "I'm so lonely and unhappy!" he wailed. He realised that there was only one thing to do. He ran down to the garden shed, picked up the lamp and rubbed it.

"You don't look very happy," said the genie, giving him a concerned glance. "What is your wish?"

"I wish everything was back to normal," Billy blurted out, "and I wish I could have no more wishes!"

"A wise choice!" said the genie. "So be it. Goodbye, Billy!" And with that the genie vanished. Billy stepped out of the shed, and from then on everything was normal again. His parents cared for him, he went to school and his friends came to play once more. But Billy had learned his lesson. He never boasted again and he always shared his sweets and toys.

The Chocolate Soldier

In the window of Mrs Brown's sweet shop there stood a chocolate soldier. He had chocolate ears, chocolate eyebrows and a curly chocolate moustache of which he was particularly proud. But best of all he loved his shiny foil uniform with its braid on the shoulders and cuffs, and smart red stripes down each leg. All day long the chocolate soldier stood to attention on a shelf in the window, staring straight ahead out into the street. Standing next to him on the shelf were more chocolate soldiers, and beyond them he could see some sugar mice and a twist of liquorice bootlaces.

It was summer time and the sun shone through the window of the sweet shop. At first the chocolate soldier felt pleasantly warm; then he started to feel uncomfortably hot. Next he began to feel most peculiar indeed. His chocolate moustache was wilting and his arms were dripping. Soon he was completely melted and before he knew it, he had slipped out through a hole in his silver foil shoe and was pouring off the shelf and out into the street.

Down the street he poured.

"Stop! Help!" he shouted, but nobody heard his cries. Now he could hear the sound of gushing water and, to his horror, he could see he was heading for a stream at the bottom of the street.

"Help me! I can't swim! I'm going to drown!" the chocolate soldier cried as he plunged into the cold, running water. But now something very strange was happening. He found he could swim quite easily. He looked round and saw that he had a chocolate tail covered in scales. He looked down at his arms, but there was a pair of fins instead. The cold water had hardened him into the shape of a chocolate fish!

The chocolate soldier was carried downstream, and after a while the stream broadened out and became a river. He realised that he would soon be carried out to sea.

57

"Whatever shall I do?" wondered the chocolate soldier. "I'm sure to get eaten by a bigger fish or maybe even a shark!" He tried to turn around and swim against the river's flow but it was no good. The current swept him away down river again.

Soon he could see the waves on the shore. He smelt the sea air and tasted the salt in the water. Now he found himself bobbing up and down on the sea. He could see a boat not far away and then all of a sudden he felt a net closing around him. He struggled to get out, but the net only tightened and soon he felt himself being hauled out of the water and landed with a "thwack!" on the deck among a pile of fish. The smell was awful, and the chocolate soldier was quite relieved when he felt the boat being rowed towards the shore.

"I'll hop over the side as soon as we land and run away," he thought, quite forgetting that he had no legs but only a fish's tail.

But there was no chance of escape. As soon as the boat reached the shore, he and all the other fish were flung into buckets and lifted into a van. The van stopped outside a shop and a man carried the buckets inside, where it smelt of fried fish,

58

chips and vinegar. The chocolate soldier found himself being lifted up with a lot of other fish in a huge metal basket. He looked down and saw a terrible sight below. They were heading for a vat of boiling oil! At that very moment he felt very peculiar once again. His scales melted, his tail drooped and he felt himself slide through the holes in the basket and into the pocket of a man's overalls.

The chocolate soldier lay in the corner of the pocket, while the man worked all day in the shop. Then the man headed for home, with the chocolate soldier bouncing up and down in the overall pocket as the man walked along. Soon they arrived at the man's house. He reached into his pocket.

"Look what I've found," he said to his small son. "A coin. Here, you can have it – but don't spend it all at once!" he said, chuckling to himself. The chocolate soldier felt himself being passed from one hand to another.

"So now I've hardened into the shape of a chocolate coin," he thought. "And I'm going to be eaten by the boy!" But to his surprise he found himself being slipped into the boy's pocket.

The chocolate soldier felt himself bouncing up and down in the child's pocket as he ran up the street and into a shop. The chocolate soldier peeped out and to his astonishment saw that he was back in Mrs Brown's sweet shop. Then he realised what was happening. The boy believed he was a real coin and was going to try and spend him! The boy stood in the queue at the counter.

The chocolate soldier called out to his soldier friends in the window, "Pssst! It's me! Help me get out of here!" One of the soldiers looked down, but all he could see was a chocolate coin sticking out of the boy's pocket. Then he recognised the voice.

"I'm a chocolate soldier like you, but I've been turned into a coin. Help!" cried the chocolate soldier.

"Leave it to me," replied the soldier on the shelf. "Don't worry, we'll have you out of there in a jiffy!"

The word was passed along and, quick as a flash, one of the sugar mice chewed off a length of liquorice bootlace. Then the soldier lowered the lace into the boy's pocket, where it stuck to the chocolate coin. Carefully the soldiers hauled the coin up on to the shelf. The chocolate soldier was delighted to find his foil uniform was still there on the shelf, just where it had been before. All the effort of getting on to the shelf had made him quite warm, and he found he could slip quite easily back through the hole in the shoe and into his uniform again.

"I'd like a chocolate soldier," said the boy to Mrs Brown. But when he reached in his pocket the coin had gone.

"Never mind," said kind Mrs Brown, "I'll let you have one anyway." She reached into the window and took down a soldier from the end of the row and gave it to the boy. And as for our chocolate soldier? In the cool of the night he turned back into a smart-looking soldier again.

The Giant Who Shrank

Once upon a time in a far-off land, there lived a huge giant.
He made his home in a big cave high up in the mountains.
His bed, table and chairs were made from great tree trunks.
And when he wanted a drink, he simply filled an old bath tub
with water and drank it down in one enormous gulp.
When he snored – which he did almost every night –
it sounded like a huge thunderstorm,
and the noise echoed all
around the mountains.

At the bottom of the mountains there was a village, but all the folk in the village were very different from the giant, for they were not big at all. They were just like you and me. They were afraid of the giant, of course, and whenever he came striding down the mountains to hunt, they all ran away into the woods or locked themselves inside their houses. Sometimes, the clumsy giant would tramp around the village squashing houses with his great feet as he went, and that only made the village folk even more frightened of him!

63

Although the giant was so big and strong, he was not a bad giant, but he was very, very lonely because everyone ran away whenever he appeared. Sometimes, while he was sitting alone in his cave, he could hear the villagers having feasts and parties and he longed to join them and be just like them.

One day, when the giant was tramping around the village as usual, something glinting in the sun caught his eye. At the top of a big tree (which of course was not very big as far as the giant was concerned) lay a gold box.

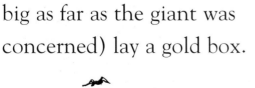

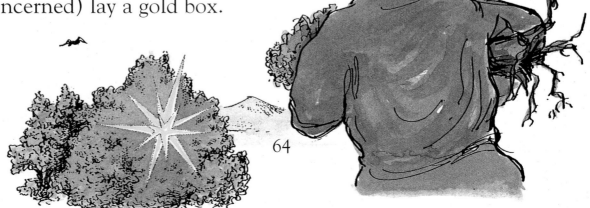

64

The giant bent down and picked up the box. To his surprise he heard a small voice inside say, "Help! Help! Let me out!"

The giant opened the box and out jumped an elf. "Thank you, thank you, large sir," he said. "I am a magic elf, but one of my spells went wrong and I got locked inside this box. No-one in the village could hear me calling for help high up in this tree."

To show his thanks, the elf said he would grant the giant one wish.

"I wish I could be the same as all the other villagers," boomed the giant.

"What a difficult wish," said the elf. "You are so big! But I will do my best." The elf closed his eyes and chanted a magic spell. But nothing seemed to happen – the giant was still as big as ever.

The giant was very sad to
discover that he had not shrunk,
but he wished the elf well, thanked
him for trying and went on his way.
As the giant was walking back to his
cave in the mountains, he noticed
something strange. All the puddles
of water that he had passed on the
way down to the village had got
bigger. They were as big as lakes
now! The giant looked up to see if
it had been raining, but the sky
was clear and blue.

Then another strange thing
happened. The big stone steps
he had cut in the mountain side
leading up to his cave had also
got bigger! He could hardly
clamber up them.

Eventually, puffing and panting,
the giant reached the door to his
cave. But he could not reach the
door knob. It now towered
above him, far from his reach.

66

"What is happening?" thought the giant. "The elf's spell must have gone wrong. Not only am I still a giant, but everything around me has now got even bigger."

Suddenly the truth came to him. Of course! Everything had not become bigger – he had become smaller! The spell had worked after all. Now he was just the same as the other folk in the village.

He made his way to the village, wondering if everyone would still run away as before. But he need not have worried. All the village folk welcomed him into the village, and he lived there happily among them for the rest of his days.

67

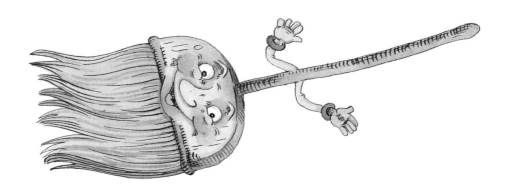

The Naughty Broom

"Goodness me, what a lot of dirt and dust there is all over this kitchen floor," said the maid. She was a very house-proud maid, and didn't like dirt and dust on her floor one little bit. Out came the broom from its place in the cupboard in the corner, and soon the maid was busily sweeping the floor and brushing all the dirt and dust into a big dustpan.

Unfortunately, this kitchen also had elves living in it. They were too tiny to see, of course, but if you upset them they could be very mischievous indeed. As the broom worked away, it swept into one dark corner where the elves were having a party. Suddenly the king elf was swept away from their little table and into the dustpan! The next thing he knew he was being thrown, with all the other rubbish, on to the rubbish tip.

Coughing and spluttering with rage, the king elf finally climbed out from under all the rubbish in the rubbish tip and stood on top of it. He picked the dirt and dust out of his ears and nose, pulled a fish bone from out of his trousers and tried to look as king-like as he could, having just been thrown on to a rubbish tip. "Who did this?" he squeaked at the top of his voice. "I'll make someone very, very sorry indeed," he vowed.

Eventually he made his way back to the house, and into the kitchen again. The other elves looked at the king elf and did their best not to laugh. For the king elf was still looking very dirty and untidy, and still had bits of rubbish stuck all over him. But the other elves knew better than to laugh at the king, because he was likely to cast a bad spell on them if they did.

"It was the broom that did it," chorused all the other elves.

"Right," said the king elf, "then I'm going to cast a bad spell on the broom."

The broom was by now back in its cupboard. The king elf marched over to the cupboard and jumped in through the keyhole. The king elf pointed to the broom and said,

"Bubble, bubble, gubble, gubble,

Go and cause a lot of trouble!"

And with that the broom suddenly stood to attention, its bristles quivering. It was night time now and everyone in the house was asleep. The broom opened its cupboard door and sprang into the kitchen. It then unlocked the kitchen door and went outside. Straight to the rubbish tip it went, and with a flick of its bristles, swept a huge pile of rubbish back into the kitchen. Tin cans, dirt, dust, chicken bones and goodness knows what else all got swept on to the kitchen floor. The broom then closed the kitchen door, took itself back to its cupboard and all was quiet until morning.

70

When the maid came down into the kitchen, she couldn't believe her eyes. "Who has made this awful mess?" she said. "If I find out it was those cats . . ." she threatened. She took the broom from the cupboard and swept all the rubbish back outside again.

The next night, the same thing happened. Once it was quiet and everyone in the house was asleep, out of its cupboard came the broom, and into the house came all the rubbish again, swept there as before by the naughty broom. This time, there were fish heads, old bottles and all the soot from the fireplaces.

Well, the maid was speechless. After clearing up again, she got the gardener to burn all the rubbish from the rubbish tip, so that nothing else could be brought in – although she still had no idea how it had happened.

That very night, the naughty broom decided it would make a mess in a different way. So instead of sweeping in rubbish from outside, the broom flew up to the shelves and knocked all the jars to the ground. With a crash they fell to the floor, one after another, and spread their contents everywhere.

"Stop this AT ONCE!" demanded a voice suddenly.

The broom stopped its mischief.

"What do you think you are doing?" said the voice again. The voice had come from a very stern-looking fairy who was now standing on the draining board, with her hands on her hips. What the broom did not know was that one of the bottles it had knocked down contained a good fairy, imprisoned by the elves. Now she was at last free, the spell was broken and it was her turn to cast a spell.

72

THE NAUGHTY BROOM

"Broom, broom, sweep this floor,
Make it cleaner than ever before.
Find the elves that cast your spell,
And sweep them off into the well," she chanted.

The broom went to work. It seemed to sweep so fast that its bristles just became a blur. Into this corner it went, then into that, and into every nook and cranny it swept. Every bit of dirt and dust, and all the broken bottles, were swept into the dustpan and then out of the house. Then it came back and swept all the elves down into the well where they couldn't do any more mischief.

In the morning, the maid came down to find a spotlessly clean kitchen. She was puzzled to find some of the jars missing, but between you and me she was also rather pleased. It just meant that there were fewer things to dust.

73

The Sad Clown

Bongo the clown had a bit of a problem. Clowns were supposed to be happy, funny, jolly people, but Bongo was a very sad clown. Nothing at all seemed to make him laugh.

Whenever the circus came to town people from all around flocked to the big top hoping for an exciting day out. They thrilled to the daring performance of the high-wire act, as the acrobats leaped from one swinging trapeze to the next. They enjoyed the jugglers, who tossed bright, sparkling balls into the air while standing on one leg. And the crowd delighted in seeing the beautiful white horses parading around the circus ring with the bareback riders balancing on their backs. When the seals came on, there was always a big cheer from the crowd, for everyone loved them and could watch their clever antics for hours.

But the biggest favourite of the crowd, especially with all the children, was the clown. Dressed in his big baggy trousers he would enter the circus ring with his funny walk. Everyone laughed to see him. They laughed even more when they saw his big floppy hat with the revolving flower on it. Even his painted clown face made them laugh.

But when his act started, the crowd thought they would burst with laughter. First of all his bicycle fell apart as he tried to ride around the ring. Then he fell out of his motor car when the seat tipped up. By the time he had accidentally poured cold water down his trousers and fallen into the custard-filled swimming pool, the crowd were almost crying with laughter.

But beneath all the makeup, Bongo the sad clown wasn't smiling at all. In fact, he saw nothing funny at all in bicycles that fell apart as you used them, or cars that tipped you out as you went along, or having cold water poured down your trousers, or even ending up face first in a swimming pool full of custard. He simply hadn't got a sense of humour.

All the other performers in the circus decided they would try and cheer the sad clown up.

"I know," said the high-wire trapeze acrobat, "let's paint an even funnier face on him. That'll make him laugh."

So that's what they did, but Bongo still didn't laugh and was still just as sad.

"Let us perform some of our tricks, just for him," said the seals.
So they sat on their stools and tossed their big coloured balls
to each other, clapped their flippers together and made lots of
honking sounds. But Bongo still didn't laugh. In fact, nothing
that anyone tried made poor Bongo smile. He was still a very
sad clown.

Then Percival the ring master spoke. "You know, I think
I know what the problem is," he said. "There is nothing a clown
likes better than playing tricks on other clowns. Perhaps if we
had a second clown, that would cheer Bongo up."

So right away they hired another clown, called Piffle.

The circus arrived in the next town and soon it was time for Bongo and Piffle's act. Piffle started riding around on his bike while Bongo pretended to wash the car by throwing a bucket of water over it. Instead of the water landing on the car, of course, it went all over Piffle, who just happened to be cycling past at that moment. A little smile flickered across Bongo's face at the sight of the soaking wet Piffle.

Next, Bongo and Piffle pretended to be cooking, and Bongo tripped while carrying two huge custard pies. Both landed right in Piffle's face. Bongo let out a huge chuckle of laughter when he saw Piffle's custard-covered face.

At the end of their act, the clowns were pretending to be decorators, painting up a ladder. Of course, you've guessed it. The ladders fell down and all the pots of paint landed on the two clowns. Bongo looked across at Piffle, who had a big paint pot stuck on his head, with paint dripping down his body. Bongo threw back his head and roared with laughter. Piffle thought Bongo looked just as funny with paint all over his body, too. And as for the crowd – well, they thought two clowns were even funnier than one and they clapped and cheered and filled the big top with laughter. After that Bongo was never a sad clown again.

The Bee Who Wanted More Stripes

Bertie the bee was a rather vain young bee. Every morning, as soon as he woke up, he would find a large dewdrop in which to admire his reflection. The thing that Bertie liked best about himself was his stripes. He thought stripes were the smartest, flashiest fashion accessory any animal could have. He just wished he had more stripes. But he only had a couple. "Still," he thought, "they are very fine stripes."

Then he had an idea. What if he could get some more stripes? He would be the stripiest bee around, and then everyone else would admire him, too. "I know what I'll do," he said. "I'll ask some other very stripy animals how they got all their stripes, and maybe I can copy them."

He buzzed off through the wood, looking for striped animals to ask. He flew across the fields and then the sea and at last he reached a place where there seemed to be quite a few striped animals. The first animal he approached looked like a striped horse. "Hello, neddy!" said Bertie, landing on the beast's nose.

"I'm not a horse – I'm a zebra. And get off my nose!" said the zebra crossly.

"I do beg your pardon," said Bertie. "I just wanted to ask you how you got your stripes."

"Well," said the zebra, "I used to be all brown. Then one day I came across a piano in the middle of the plain. As I walked past the piano, its black and white keys started to play a tune all by themselves. Then I looked down and found I had turned black and white, too. And if you believe that you'll believe anything!" And with that the zebra laughed and trotted off.

Bertie continued on his way. Now he could see a large striped cat. "Hello, puss!" said Bertie, landing on the creature's back.

"I'm not a cat – I'm a tiger. And get off my back!" growled the tiger.

"I'm so sorry," said Bertie, "I just wanted to ask you how you got your stripes."

"Well," said the tiger, "I used to be all yellow. Then one day, when I was a cub, I was playing with a ball of black string and I got all tangled up in it. And that's how I got my stripes. And if you believe that you'll believe anything!" And the tiger started to laugh as he stalked off.

Bertie continued on his way. Soon he could see a long striped worm slithering through the grass. "Hello, little worm!" called Bertie, landing on the worm's tail.

"I'm not a worm – I'm a snake. And get off my tail!" hissed the snake.

"Oh dear. I didn't mean to upset you," said Bertie. "I just wanted to ask you how you got your stripes."

"Well," said the snake, "I used to be all brown. Then one day I was crossing a road just as the traffic lights were changing from red to green, and when I reached the other side I found that I was striped red and green from head to tail. And if you believe that you'll believe anything!" And the snake started to laugh as he slithered away.

Bertie continued on his way once more. Then he spotted a squirrel with a striped tail in a tree. "Hello, squirrel!" he said, landing on the animal's paw.

"I'm not a squirrel – I'm a ring-tailed lemur. And get off my paw!" said the ring-tailed lemur angrily.

"I do apologise," said Bertie. "I just wanted to ask you how you got your striped tail."

"Well," said the ring-tailed lemur, "my tail used to be all white. Then one day I was playing hoop-la with my friends. I said they could use my tail as a target, and so they threw all the rings on to my tail. But they got stuck. And that's how I got a striped tail. And if you believe that you'll believe anything!" And the ring-tailed lemur started to laugh as he scampered away.

"Well," thought Bertie, "I'd better give it a go!" First he looked for a piano on the plain, but to no avail. There just wasn't a piano to be found. Then he looked for a ball of string – but he couldn't find one of those, either. He did find a set of traffic lights and he buzzed backwards and forwards in front of them until he felt quite dizzy, but he still had the same number of stripes. Finally, he called out, "Anyone fancy a game of hoop-la?" But there was no reply. It was night time and all the animals were asleep.

"I'll just have to make my way home," thought Bertie sadly. He flew all through the night and arrived home exhausted in the morning.

Just then he met Clarice, the wise old bee. "Clarice," said Bertie, "I really would like some more stripes, but although I've asked lots of stripy animals how they got their stripes, all they gave me were silly answers."

Clarice looked at Bertie rather sternly and said, "You only get the stripes you were born with, Bertie. And besides, do you know what you would be if you had more stripes? You would be a wasp!"

Bertie looked horrified. The last thing he wanted to be was a wasp. Wasps were always going around frightening and stinging everyone, and no-one liked them at all.

Bertie thought for a few moments and then said, "Perhaps having just a few stripes but being liked by others is better after all."

Little Red Riding Hood

There was once a little girl who was given a lovely, bright red cloak by her grandmother. The little girl loved this cloak very much. She loved it so much in fact that she never wanted to take it off, and was always wearing it. Because of this, she became known as Little Red Riding Hood.

One sunny morning, Little Red Riding Hood's mother asked her if she would take some cakes and apple juice to her grandmother, who was ill.

Little Red Riding Hood loved her grandmother very much, and was pleased to be going to visit her.

"But don't delay," said Little Red Riding Hood's mother, "go straight to your grandmother's house and don't play in the forest on the way."

Little Red Riding Hood promised to do as she was told, and said goodbye to her mother and set off.

On the way to her grandmother's house, Little Red Riding Hood met a wolf walking through the forest. Now Little Red Riding Hood did not know that he was wicked, and so she said, "Good morning, Mr Wolf."

"Well, good morning, Little Red Riding Hood," replied the wolf, "and where are you going?"

"I am going to visit my grandmother, who is ill in bed," said Little Red Riding Hood.

87

"What have you got in your basket, Little Red Riding Hood?" asked the wolf.

"I've got some cakes and a jug of apple juice," said Little Red Riding Hood.

"And where does your grandmother live?" asked the wolf.

"She lives in the forest, not far from here," said Little Red Riding Hood. "Her house is easy to find. It's right next to the lake."

Now the reason that the wolf was asking all these questions was because he really wanted to gobble up Little Red Riding Hood and her grandmother. Suddenly he thought of a cunning plan. "Little Red Riding Hood," he said, "I have an idea! Why don't you pick some of those beautiful flowers which are growing in the forest and give them to your sick grandmother?"

"What a good idea," said Little Red Riding Hood. "My grandmother would be so pleased to have some of these pretty flowers. I'm sure they would make her feel better."

And with that, she set about picking a big bunch of the prettiest flowers she could find. In fact, she was so busy looking for flowers that she didn't see the crafty wolf skip away and make off towards her grandmother's house. The wolf soon came to the house, and knocked on the door.

"Who is it?" said Grandmother.

"It's me, Little Red Riding Hood," said the wolf. "I've brought you some cakes and a jug of apple juice."

"Come in, come in, my dear," said Grandmother, "the door isn't locked."

The wolf then went into the house, and as soon as he saw the old lady lying in bed, he ran straight over to her and gobbled her up. Next he put on her nightdress and her frilly night cap and jumped into her bed, pulling the bed clothes up to his chin.

In a little while, Little Red Riding Hood – who had by now picked a lovely bunch of flowers for her grandmother – came hurrying up the garden path. The door to her grandmother's house was still open and so she went inside and walked over to the bed. Little Red Riding Hood could only see a little bit of her face poking out from the bed clothes.

"My, Grandmother, what big ears you have," said Little Red Riding Hood.

90

LITTLE RED RIDING HOOD

"All the better to hear you with, my dear," said the wolf.

"My, Grandmother, what big eyes you have," said Little Red Riding Hood.

"All the better to see you with, my dear," said the wolf.

"My, Grandmother, what big hands you have," said Little Red Riding Hood.

"All the better to hold you tight with, my dear," said the wolf.

"My, Grandmother, what big teeth you have," said Little Red Riding Hood.

"All the better to eat you with, my dear," cried the wolf. And with that he jumped out of bed and gobbled her up.

The wolf felt very full and rather sleepy after he had eaten Little Red Riding Hood. After all, he'd already just eaten her grandmother, too. So he went back to bed and fell asleep, snoring loudly.

Just then, a hunter was passing the house and heard the snoring. He looked through the window, and when he saw the wolf lying in bed, he realised that the wolf must have eaten the old lady. So, while the wolf was still sleeping, the hunter took his knife and cut open the wolf's stomach. To the hunter's great surprise, out popped Little Red Riding Hood and her grandmother. Luckily, the hunter had arrived just in time and both were still alive.

Little Red Riding Hood and her grandmother both thanked the hunter for saving them, and the hunter took the dead wolf's skin and went home.

Little Red Riding Hood's grandmother ate the cakes and drank the apple juice, and soon she was feeling much better. And Little Red Riding Hood? Well, she decided that she would never talk to a wolf again!

Buried Treasure

Jim lived in a big old house with a big rambling garden. The house was rather spooky, and Jim much preferred the garden. He would spend hours kicking a football around the overgrown lawn, climbing the old apple trees in the orchard or just staring into the pond in case he might spot a fish. It was a wonderful garden to play in but Jim was not really a happy child because he was lonely. How he wished he had someone to play with! It would be such fun to play football with a friend, or have someone to go fishing with. He had plenty of friends at school, but it was a long bus journey to his home and besides, his school friends found his house so spooky that they only came to visit once.

One day Jim was hunting about in the garden with a stick. He hoped he might find some interesting small creatures to examine. Every time he found a new creature he would draw it and try to find out its name. So far, he had discovered eight types of snails and six different ladybirds. As he was poking about under some leaves he saw a piece of metal sticking out of the ground. He reached down and pulled it free. In his hand lay a rusty old key. It was quite big, and as Jim brushed away the soil, he saw that it was carved with beautiful patterns.

Jim carried the key indoors and cleaned it and polished it. Then he set about trying to find the lock that it fitted. First he tried the old garden gate that had been locked as long as Jim could remember. But the key was far too small. Next he tried the grandfather clock in the hall. But the key did not fit the clock's lock. Then he remembered an old wind-up teddy bear that played the drum. Jim hadn't played with the toy for a long time and he eagerly tried out the key, but this time it was too big.

Then Jim had another idea. "Perhaps the key fits something in the attic," he thought. He was usually too scared to go into the attic on his own because it really was scary. But now he was so determined to find the key's home that he ran up the stairs boldly and opened the door. The attic was dimly lit, dusty and full of cobwebs. The water pipes hissed and creaked and Jim shivered. He began to look under a few dustsheets and opened some old boxes, but didn't find anything that looked like it needed a key to unlock it. Then he caught sight of a large book sticking out from one of the shelves. It was one of those sorts of books fitted with a lock. Jim lifted down the book, which was extremely heavy, and put it on the floor. His fingers trembled as he put the key in the lock. It fitted perfectly. He turned the key and the lock sprang open, releasing a cloud of dust. Jim wiped the dust from his eyes, slowly opened the book and turned the pages.

What a disappointment! The pages were crammed with tiny writing and there were no pictures at all. Jim was about to shut the book again when he heard a voice. The voice was coming from the book! "You have unlocked my secrets," it said. "Step into my pages if you are looking for adventure."

Jim was so curious that he found himself stepping on to the book. As soon as he put his foot on the pages he found himself falling through the book. The next thing he knew he was on the deck of a ship. He looked up and saw a tattered black flag flying from a flagpole and on the flag were a skull and crossbones. He was on a pirate ship! He looked down and saw that he was dressed like a pirate.

The pirate ship was sailing along nicely, when suddenly Jim saw some dangerous-looking rocks in the water – and they were heading straight for them! Before he could shout, the ship had run aground and all the pirates were jumping overboard and swimming to the shore. Jim swam, too.

The water felt deliciously warm and when he reached the shore he found warm sand between his toes. He couldn't believe it! Here he was on a desert island. The pirates went in all directions, searching for something to make a shelter. Jim looked, too, and under a rock he found a book. The book looked familiar to Jim. He was sure he'd seen it somewhere before. He was still puzzling over it when one of the pirates came running towards him waving a knife. "You thief, you stole me rubies!" cursed the pirate in a menacing voice. What was Jim to do?

Then he heard a voice call out from the book, "Quick! Step into my pages." Without thinking twice, Jim stepped into the book and suddenly he was back in the attic again.

Jim peered closely at the page from which he'd just stepped. *The Pirates and the Stolen Treasure* it said at the top of the page. Jim read the page and found he was reading exactly the adventure he had been in. He turned excitedly to the contents page at the front of the book and read the chapter titles. *Journey to Mars*, he read, and *The Castle Under the Sea*. Further down it said: *The Magic Car* and *Into the Jungle*. Jim was thrilled. He realised that he could open the book at any page and become part of the adventure, and he only had to find the book and step into it to get back to the attic again.

After that, Jim had many, many adventures. He made lots of friends in the stories and he had lots of narrow escapes. But he always found the book again just in time. Jim was never lonely again.

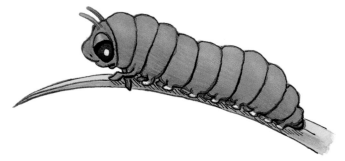

The Jealous Caterpillar

One spring day a green caterpillar sat on a leaf. He watched a beautiful butterfly flutter past him on the breeze. "It's not fair. Here I am stuck on this boring leaf with nothing to do and nowhere to go while that lucky creature can fly across the world and see far-off lands," thought the caterpillar crossly. "And what's more," he continued to himself, "not only has that butterfly got wings with which to fly, but he's beautiful, too. Look at poor me. I'm just a dull green. No-one will notice me because I'm the same colour as the leaf." The caterpillar really did feel very sorry for himself, and rather jealous. "Go and enjoy yourself. Don't worry about me," he called spitefully to the butterfly.

100

But the butterfly hadn't heard a single word the caterpillar had been muttering, and soon he flew away. The caterpillar suddenly decided that he was going to be like the butterfly. "I'll learn how to fly and I'll paint myself lovely colours so that I look beautiful, too," he thought. He looked around for something to paint himself with but, of course, there was nothing at all on the leaf. Then he tried to fly. He launched himself from his leaf and tried to flap his tail, but all he did was land on the leaf below.

Along came a ladybird. "Aha!" thought the caterpillar. "Here's a beautiful creature who knows how to fly. I'll ask her to teach me." So the caterpillar said, "Hello, I've been admiring your beautiful wingcase. Could you tell me how I, too, could be beautiful? And can you teach me to fly?"

The ladybird looked at the caterpillar. "Be patient and wait a while," she said wisely, "and soon enough you'll get what you want." And with that the ladybird went on her way.

101

"Whatever can she mean? She's just too proud to teach me," the caterpillar thought jealously.

Some time later a bee buzzed past and landed on a nearby leaf. "Aha!" thought the caterpillar. "Here's a beautiful creature who knows how to fly. I'll ask him to teach me." So the caterpillar said, "Hello, I've been admiring your beautiful striped back. Could you tell me how I, too, could be beautiful? And can you teach me to fly?"

The bee looked at the caterpillar. "You'll find out soon enough, young man," said the bee sternly. And with that he went on his way.

"Whatever can he mean? He's just too haughty to teach me," the caterpillar thought jealously.

Now a while later along came a bird. "Aha!" thought the caterpillar once more. "Here's a beautiful creature who knows how to fly. I'll ask him to teach me." So once again the caterpillar said, "Hello, I've been admiring your beautiful feathers. Could you tell me how I, too, could be beautiful? And can you teach me to fly?"

The bird looked at the caterpillar and thought to himself slyly that here was a very silly caterpillar, but he would make a tasty snack for his chicks. "Let's see if I can trick him," he thought.

"I can't give you wings and I can't make you beautiful. But I can show you the world. I expect you'd like to see the world, wouldn't you, little caterpillar?" said the bird.

"Oh, yes!" said the caterpillar in great excitement.

"Climb upon my back then, little caterpillar!" said the crafty bird.

103

The caterpillar did as he was told and the bird flew off towards his nest. At first the caterpillar clung tightly to the bird's back but soon he felt quite sleepy and eventually he dozed off and slipped from the bird's back. Down he fell through the air and landed on a leaf, but still he didn't wake up. Soon he was wrapped in a soft, brown, papery cocoon from which he would not wake up for a long while.

Meanwhile, the bird reached his nest. "Look at the treat I've brought you," he said to his chicks.

They looked very puzzled. "What treat, Dad?" one of them piped up.

"This nice juicy caterpillar," said the bird, shaking the feathers on his back. "Climb down, little caterpillar," he said. But of course there was nothing there. Now it was the father's turn to look puzzled, while the chicks laughed at him.

104

"Well, I must have dropped him," he said. "I've never done that before," he added. He flew out of the nest in search of the caterpillar but he was nowhere to be seen. Once he saw a strange brown, papery parcel on a leaf, but in the end the bird had to return to the nest with his beak empty.

A long while later the caterpillar woke up. "I must get out of this stuffy wrapping," he thought, as he pushed his way out. He stood on the leaf and yawned and stretched. As he stretched, he noticed to his amazement two pairs of beautiful wings spreading out on either side of his body. "Are they really mine?" he wondered. He tried lifting and turning them and yes, he could make them work. He looked at his reflection in a raindrop and saw a lovely butterfly staring back at him. "So the ladybird and the bee were right," he exclaimed. "How foolish I was to be a jealous caterpillar," he declared to a passing ant, "for now I am a beautiful butterfly after all."

Peter Meets a Dragon

Once upon a time there was a young boy named Peter. He lived in an ordinary house with an ordinary Mum and Dad, an ordinary sister and an ordinary pet cat, called Jasper. In fact, everything in Peter's life was so ordinary that he sometimes wished that something extraordinary would happen. "Why doesn't a giant come and squash the house flat with his foot?" he wondered, and "If only a pirate would take my sister hostage!" But each day, Peter would wake up in the morning and everything was just the same as it had been the day before.

One morning Peter woke up to find a very strange smell in the house. Looking out of his bedroom window, he saw that the front lawn was scorched and blackened. There was smoke drifting off the grass and, further away, he could see some bushes ablaze.

Peter rushed downstairs and out of the front door. He ran out of the garden and down the lane following the trail of smoke and burning grass. He grew more and more puzzled, however, as there was no sign of anything that could have caused such a blaze.

Peter was about to run home and tell his Mum and Dad, when he heard a panting noise coming from the undergrowth. Parting the bushes gently with his hands he found a young creature. It had green, scaly skin, a pair of wings and a long snout full of sharp teeth. Every now and again a little tongue of flame came from its nostrils, setting the grass around it on fire. "A baby dragon!" Peter said to himself, in great surprise. Big tears were rolling out of the dragon's yellow eyes and down its scaly cheeks as it flapped its wings desperately and tried to take off.

When the dragon saw Peter it stopped flapping its wings. "Oh, woe is me!" it sobbed. "Where am I?"

"Where do you want to be?" asked Peter, kneeling down on the scorched ground.

107

"I want to be in Dragonland with my friends," replied the dragon. "We were all flying together, but I just couldn't keep up with them. I got tired and needed a rest. I called to the others but they didn't hear me. Then I just had to stop and get my breath back. Now I don't know where I am, or if I'll ever see my friends again!" And with that the baby dragon started to cry once more.

"I'm sure I can help. I'll get you home," said Peter, though he had no idea how.

"You?" hissed a voice nearby. "How could you possibly help? You're just a boy!" Peter looked round, and to his astonishment found Jasper sitting behind him. "I suppose you're going to wave a magic wand, are you?" continued Jasper. "You need to call in an expert." Then he turned his back on Peter and the baby dragon and started washing his paws.

Peter was astounded. He'd never heard Jasper talking before. He had thought he was just an ordinary pet cat. "W… w… what do you mean?" he stammered.

"Well," said Jasper, glancing over his shoulder at Peter, "I reckon that horse over there could help. Follow me."

108

So Peter and the baby dragon – whose name was Flame – followed Jasper over to where the horse stood at the edge of a field. Jasper leaped up on to the gate and called to the horse. Then he whispered in the horse's ear. The horse thought for a moment, then whispered back in Jasper's ear. "He says he's got a friend on the other side of the wood who'll help," said Jasper.

"But how?" said Peter, looking perplexed.

"Be patient! Follow me!" said Jasper as he stalked off through the grass. "And tell your friend to stop setting fire to everything!" he added. Peter saw, to his horror, that Flame was indeed blazing a trail through the field.

"I can't help it," cried Flame, about to burst into tears again. "Every time I get out of breath I start to pant, and then I start breathing fire."

"Let me carry you," said Peter. He picked Flame up in his arms and ran after Jasper. The baby dragon felt very strange. His body was all cold and clammy, but his mouth was still breathing hot smoke, which made Peter's eyes water.

He ran through the wood, just keeping Jasper's upright tail in sight. On the other side of the wood was another field, and in the field was a horse. But this was no ordinary horse. Peter stopped dead in his tracks and stared. The horse was pure milky white, and from its head grew a single, long horn. "A unicorn!" breathed Peter.

Jasper was already talking to the unicorn. He beckoned with his paw to Peter. "He'll take your friend home and you can go, too, Peter, but don't be late for tea, or you know what your mother will say." And with that, Jasper was off.

"Climb aboard," said the unicorn gently.

Peter and the little dragon scrambled up on to the unicorn's back. "What an adventure," thought Peter. Up, up, and away they soared through the clouds.

Flame held tightly on to Peter's hand with his clammy paw. At last Peter could see a mountain ahead through the clouds. Now they were descending through the clouds again, and soon the unicorn landed right at the top of the mountain. "I'm home!" squeaked Flame joyously as they landed. Sure enough, several dragons were running over to greet him. They looked quite friendly, but some of them were rather large and one was breathing a great deal of fire.

"Time for me to go," said Peter a little nervously, as Flame jumped off the unicorn's back and flew to the ground. The unicorn took off again and soon they were back in the field once more.

As he slid off the unicorn's back, Peter turned to thank him, but when he looked he saw that it was just an ordinary horse with no trace of a horn at all. Peter walked back home across the field, but there was no sign of burnt grass. He reached his own front lawn, which was also in perfect condition. Peter felt more and more perplexed. "I hope Jasper can explain," he thought, as the cat ran past him and into the house. "Jasper, I took the baby dragon home. What's happened to the burnt grass?" he blurted out. But Jasper said not a word. He ignored Peter and curled up in his basket.

When Peter wasn't looking, however, Jasper gave him a glance that seemed to say, "Well, was that a big enough adventure for you?"

111

Mr Squirrel Won't Sleep

It was autumn. The leaves were falling from the trees in the forest and there was a cold nip in the air. All the animals began to get ready for winter.

One night Mr Fox came back from hunting and said to his wife, "There's not much food about now it's getting colder. We'd better start storing what we can to help tide us over the winter."

"You're right, Mr Fox," replied his wife, as she gathered her cubs into their lair.

"I'd love to go fishing," said Mr Bear, "but I'll have to wait until spring now." He went into his den, shut the door tight and sealed it.

"Well, I'm off for a holiday in the sun," announced Mrs Cuckoo, preening her feathers. "See you all next year!" she called as she took to the wing and flew south.

Mrs Mouse ran by with a mouthful of straw. "Must dash," she squeaked, "or my winter bed will never be finished in time." But soon she, too, was curled up with her tail wrapped around her for warmth.

Now only Mr Squirrel wasn't ready for winter. He danced about in his tree, leaping from branch to branch and chasing his tail. "Ha, ha!" he boasted. "I don't have to get ready for winter. I have a fine store of nuts hidden away, a beautiful bushy tail to keep me warm and besides, I don't feel in the least bit sleepy." And he carried on playing in his tree.

"Are you still awake?" snapped Mr Fox.

"Go to sleep!" growled Mr Bear.

"Please be quiet," squeaked Mrs Mouse, drawing her tail more tightly about her ears.

But Mr Squirrel wouldn't go to sleep. Not a bit of it. He danced up and down all the more and shouted, "I'm having SUCH FUN!" at the top of his voice.

Winter came. The wind whistled in the trees' bare branches, the sky turned grey and it became bitterly cold. Then it started to snow. At first Mr Squirrel had a grand time making snowballs – but there was no-one around to throw them at and he began to feel rather lonely. Soon he felt cold and hungry, too.

"No problem!" he said to himself. "I'll have some nice nuts to eat. Now, where did I bury them?" He scampered down his tree to find that the ground was deep with snow. He ran this way and that trying to find his hiding places, but all the forest looked the same in the snow and soon he was hopelessly lost.

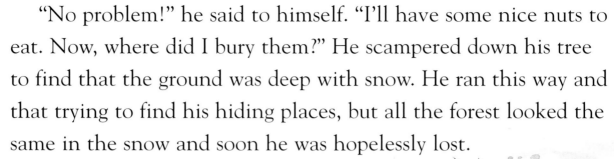

"Whatever shall I do?" he whimpered, for now he was shivering with cold and hunger and his beautiful, bushy tail was all wet and bedraggled.

All of a sudden he thought he heard a small voice. But where was it coming from? He looked all around but there was no sign of anyone. Then he realised that the voice was coming from under the snow. "Hurry up!" said the voice. "You can join me down here, but you'll have to dig a path to my door."

Mr Squirrel started digging frantically with his front paws and sure enough there was a path leading to a door under a tree stump. The door was slightly open – open enough for Mr Squirrel to squeeze his thin, tired body through.

Inside was a warm, cosy room with a roaring fire, and sitting by the fire was a tiny elf. "I heard you running around up there and thought you might be in need of a bit of shelter," said the elf. "Come and warm yourself by the fire." Mr Squirrel was only too pleased to accept and soon he was feeling warm and dry.

"This isn't my house, you know," said the elf. "I think it might part of an old badgers' sett. I got lost in the forest and so when found this place, I decided to stay here until spring. Though how I'll ever find my way home, I don't know." A fat tear rolled down the elf's cheek.

"I have been a very foolish squirrel," said Mr Squirrel. "If you hadn't taken me in I surely would have died. I am indebted to you and if you will let me stay here until spring, I will help you find your way home."

"Of course you can stay," replied the elf. "I'd be glad of the company." So Mr Squirrel settled down with his tail for a blanket and soon he was fast asleep.

Days and nights passed, until one day the elf popped his head out of the door and exclaimed, "The snow has melted, spring is coming. Wake up, Mr Squirrel." Mr Squirrel rubbed his eyes and looked out. It was true. There were patches of blue in the sky and he could hear a bird singing.

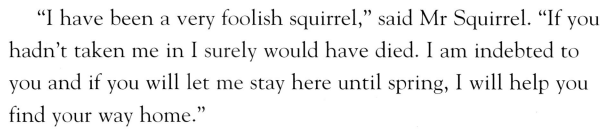

"Climb upon my back," Mr Squirrel said to the elf. "I'm going to show you the world." They set off through the forest until they came to the highest tree of all.

"Hold tight!" called Mr Squirrel as he climbed up through the branches until finally they reached the very top of the tree.

"You can look now," said Mr Squirrel, seeing that the elf had put his tiny hands over his eyes. The elf uncovered his eyes and stared and stared. He had never seen anything like it in his whole life. Stretching in all directions, as far as the eye could see, were mountains, lakes, rivers, forests and fields.

"What's that silvery-blue thing in the distance?" asked the elf.

"Why, that's the sea!" replied Mr Squirrel.

Suddenly the elf started to jump for joy.

"What is it?" said Mr Squirrel.

"I… I… can see my home," cried the elf, pointing down into the valley below the forest. "And there's my wife sitting in a chair in the sunshine. I must go home, Mr Squirrel. Thank you for showing me the world, for I should never have seen my home again without you." And with that he climbed down the tree and skipped all the way home.

Mr Squirrel made his way back to his own tree.

"Where have you been?" said Mr Fox.

"We've been looking for you," said Mr Bear.

"I'm glad you're home," said Mrs Mouse.

"So am I," said Mr Squirrel. "I've been very foolish, but I've learned my lesson. Now let's have a party – I've got rather a lot of nuts that need eating up!"

So the animals celebrated spring with a fine feast.

And Mr Squirrel vowed not to be silly again next winter.

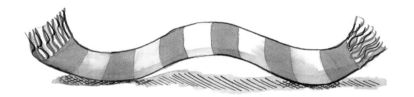

The Missing Scarf

Kanga was very proud of her stripy knitted scarf. She had made it herself and she had also made a smaller matching one for her son, Joey. Kanga used to hop through the bush with her scarf streaming out behind her, while Joey's could just be seen poking out of the top of her pouch. Now Joey was older, he was too big for Kanga's pouch, but he still wore his scarf as he hopped along beside his mother.

Then one day Kanga woke up to find that her beautiful scarf was missing. She searched high and low but it was nowhere to be found. Eventually she decided that she would have to go out into the bush to look for it.

"Stay here," she said to Joey. "I'll try not to be long. I'm sure to find my scarf soon." Kanga hopped off into the bush and started to search among the roots of trees and under stones.

She had gone quite a long way when, looking up into the branches of a eucalyptus tree, she spotted Koala. Now Koala was usually to be found asleep, but this time she was busy preparing a meal of eucalyptus leaves for her children. Kanga looked up at Koala and then her jaw dropped. For Koala was quite clearly wearing Kanga's scarf around her tummy. Then, to Kanga's horror, she saw Koala use the end of the scarf to wipe the teacups! "Koala," Kanga called. "Whatever do you think you're doing?"

Koala stopped cleaning the teacups and looked down through the branches of the eucalyptus tree at Kanga. "I'm wiping my teacups with my apron," she replied sleepily, "and I'll thank you not to interfere!" And with that, she yawned and moved several branches further up the tree.

119

Poor Kanga felt very embarrassed. How could she have mistaken Koala's striped apron for her own scarf? She hopped away and carried on further into the bush. After a while she could hear Kookaburra's familiar laughing call nearby. "I know," thought Kanga, "I'll ask her if she's seen my scarf. She'd be able to spot it easily from up in the sky." She followed the sound of Kookaburra's call until she came to the tree where she lived. She looked up and, sure enough, there was Kookaburra flying towards the tree. Kanga was about to call up when her jaw dropped again. For Kookaburra was quite clearly carrying Kanga's scarf in her beak. "Kookaburra," Kanga called. "Whatever do you think you're doing?"

"I'm lining my nest," mumbled Kookaburra through a beakful of stripy feathers. "And I'll thank you not to interfere," she added more distinctly, for she had now reached the nest and was arranging the feathers carefully in place.

120

Poor Kanga felt even more embarrassed. How could she have mistaken the feathers for her own scarf? She hopped away and carried on further into the bush. After a while she reached a wide open plain and there she saw Emu running past with his baby chicks on his back. As he rushed past, Kanga's jaw dropped yet again. For Emu quite clearly had Kanga's scarf tucked in among his chicks. "Emu," called Kanga. "Whatever do you think you're doing?"

"I'm taking my chicks to safety," said Emu, glancing up at the sky as he sped away. "And you'd be wise to do the same," he added. Then Kanga realised that what she had thought was her rolled-up scarf were just the striped chicks on Emu's back.

Poor Kanga felt even more embarrassed. How could she have made such a mistake? Then she felt a few spots of rain on her nose and, looking up, saw a huge black cloud overhead. There was no time to lose – she must find shelter.

121

She made a dash for some trees at the edge of the plain and soon found herself by a stream. She wandered along beside the stream feeling cold, wet, tired and miserable. Finally, she lay down in the wet grass beside the stream and tried to get to sleep. She shivered with cold and wondered how Joey was and whether he was behaving himself. She so hoped he hadn't got into mischief.

Just then there was a tap on her shoulder and there stood Platypus. "I could hear you in my burrow over there," she said pointing towards a hole beside the stream just above the water. "I thought you might like this to keep you warm," she added.

"My scarf!" exclaimed Kanga.

"Oh, is that what it is? I'm ever so sorry," said Platypus. "I've been using it as a blanket for my babies. It's rather cold and damp in my burrow, you know," she added, rather forlornly. "Where did you find it?" asked Kanga.

"It was stuck on some thorns and I know I shouldn't have taken it, but I just thought it would be so nice for keeping my

young ones warm," blurted Platypus, and she started to sob.

"There now," said Kanga, "don't cry. You can keep the scarf. You need it more than me."

Platypus stopped crying and looked overjoyed. "Thank you," she said.

"No, thank you," said Kanga. "I've learned a lesson, which is not to get upset over a scarf, for I've ended up falling out with my friends."

Kanga made her way back home, but it took a long time because she apologised to all her friends on the way. When she explained what had happened Emu, Kookaburra and Koala all forgave her, and by the time she reached home she was feeling much better. Joey was there to greet her. "What have you been up to while I was away?" she asked.

"I made you this," he said. He handed her a scarf. It was a very funny-looking scarf, made out of twigs, grass and feathers, but Kanga loved it very much.

"This is much more special than my old scarf," she said. And she gave Joey an extra big hug.

123

The Bear and the Ice Kingdom

Once upon a time a king ruled a far-off land. It was a sunny, pleasant kingdom with lush forests, green meadows and sparkling rivers. The king of this land had a daughter he loved very much, and who one day would rule the kingdom.

Beyond the king's land was another kingdom, but this one was very different. It was an icy-cold place with wind-swept, snowy plains and cold, frozen seas. The sun never warmed this kingdom, and it was always winter. Anyone or anything venturing into the kingdom was immediately turned to ice by the cold. This kingdom was ruled by a wicked ogre, whose wish was to own the warm lands of his neighbour.

124

One day the wicked ogre thought of a cunning plan to capture the kingdom he desired. He decided he would kidnap the king's daughter. Once she had entered the wicked ogre's ice kingdom she, too, would be turned to ice. In time, the king would die and, as there would be no-one to inherit his kingdom, the wicked ogre could seize it.

So one day, the wicked ogre left his own cold kingdom and travelled to the other kingdom disguised as a merchant. He carried a big bag containing some samples of cloth and some jewellery. The wicked ogre came to the castle gates and asked if he might show the princess his wares. She agreed, and showed him to a room where he laid out the cloth and jewellery on a table. But as soon as she started to look at the wares, the wicked ogre bundled her up in the bag and carried her off.

As soon as the princess felt the cold chill of the wicked ogre's kingdom, she was immediately frozen to ice.

The wicked ogre thought that all he now had to do was wait for the king to die of old age or a broken heart, and the kingdom would be his. But despite the cunning of the wicked ogre, his evil deed had been spotted by one of the king's courtiers. The king immediately sent his troops to the ice kingdom to rescue his daughter. But as soon as they reached the kingdom they, too, were frozen to ice.

The king was in despair. There seemed to be no way to get his beloved daughter back. Then one day he thought of an idea. He sent out a royal proclamation to every part of his land. It said that anyone who could rescue his daughter would be granted any gift within the king's power to bestow.

Many adventurers tried to rescue the king's daughter, in the hope that they might win her hand in marriage, or be granted riches and lands as a reward. But each who ventured into the evil ogre's ice kingdom met the same fate. All were turned to ice.

Then one day, the king's dancing bear read the royal proclamation and asked to speak with the king. "Your majesty," said the dancing bear, "I have a plan to rescue your daughter, the princess."

"And what is your plan?" asked the king.

"My plan is a secret, your majesty," said the dancing bear. "But if you will trust me, I promise she will be brought safely home."

The king agreed to let the dancing bear try and rescue his daughter. After all, every other attempt had ended in failure so what did he have to lose? The dancing bear was released from his chain and went off immediately to begin his task. He travelled day and night until finally he reached his destination – a cold, snowy place where his cousin lived. His cousin was not like the dancing bear, however. The dancing bear was small and brown, but his cousin was big and white. This bear loved the cold and snow, for he had a thick fur coat. He was a polar bear.

The dancing bear told his cousin what had befallen the king's daughter. The polar bear agreed to rescue her. The dancing bear couldn't wait to get going, for his cousin's snowy home was much too cold for him. Eventually they arrived back in the king's land, and the polar bear set off alone to try and rescue the princess.

Soon he reached the wicked ogre's ice kingdom. A freezing, icy wind blew all around the polar bear, but his thick, warm fur coat kept out the cold. Then a huge snow storm came up, but the polar bear just shook his fur and all the snow fell from him. On went the polar bear until he reached the wicked ogre's castle.

The ogre never expected that anyone would be able to enter his cold kingdom without being turned to ice, so he never even locked his doors. While the ogre was snoring in his bedroom, the polar bear searched stealthily around the castle until he found the frozen princess. He gently gathered her up, and they were just about to make their escape when the ogre awoke.

128

As the wicked ogre tried to snatch the princess away from the polar bear, the polar bear dealt the wicked ogre a mighty blow with his paw. The wicked ogre fell down dead. The polar bear then carried the princess away from the icy kingdom. As soon as she entered her father's warm kingdom again, she returned to life.

There was much rejoicing at the return of the king's daughter, of course, and the first thing the king did was to summon the dancing bear to him.

"You have kept you promise," the king said, "and now I will keep mine. What is your wish?"

"All I ask, your majesty, is that I am freed to roam the forests of your kingdom."

The king immediately granted his wish. And as a reward to the polar bear, he was given the ice kingdom as his own domain which, being so cold, suited him just fine!

129

Jack and the Beanstalk

Once there was an old woman who lived with her only son Jack in a tumble-down cottage in a meadow by a pine forest. The old woman and her son were very poor, and they were getting poorer as each winter passed. After one particularly cruel and cold winter, when the ground had frozen like ice, the old woman turned to her son and said, "Jack, there is only one thing left to sell. You must take the old brown cow to market tomorrow and sell her for her meat – she is all that is left between us and starvation, so mind you get a good price!"

So the next morning Jack took the old brown cow and started the long journey into town.

Halfway through his journey, Jack stopped to eat his crust of bread. Just then a farmer passed by, and stopped to chat. After Jack told the farmer where he was heading and why, the farmer looked at the old cow and scratched his chin thoughtfully. He put his hand into his pocket and said to Jack, "I'll swap you these dried beans for your old brown cow."

Jack looked at the beans in the farmer's hand and shook his head. "I'm sorry," he said, "but I must take the old brown cow to sell at the market so that my mother and I can buy bread."

The farmer promised Jack that if he would swap the cow for the beans, Jack would make his fortune. Jack finally agreed, and went home with the beans in his pocket.

When he got home he told his mother about his adventure, but his mother cried when Jack told her the old brown cow was gone and all they had were dried beans. She snatched the beans from Jack's hand and threw them out of the window in anger.

Just as dawn was breaking, Jack woke up to discover a huge beanstalk had shot up during the night right outside his window. He ran downstairs and looked at the huge beanstalk – it was taller than even the tallest trees in the nearby pine forest, and disappeared into the clouds. Jack decided to climb the beanstalk.

Jack climbed and climbed. He climbed so high that when he looked down, the tumble-down cottage was a tiny speck far below. The top of the beanstalk was still out of sight so he climbed some more. Eventually, Jack climbed through the clouds and was amazed when he got to the top of the stalk to discover another land very different from the one he'd left below.

Everything was HUGE. The trees were enormous, the grass came up to Jack's shoulder, and in the distance was the largest castle he had ever seen. Just as Jack was starting out towards the castle, he heard a thunderous rustling in the grass behind him, and he looked round to see a huge giantess towering above him.

"Mmmmm – not much meat on those bones," she said, "so I won't bother to eat you. However, you might come in handy around the house to do all the boring old chores." And with that she picked Jack up and popped him into the pocket of her apron, and carried him into the castle. On the way, she warned Jack not to let her husband, the giant, see him. "The last house boy I had was made into jam, and he's looking for another to pound into bread," she said quite calmly.

Soon Jack felt the castle shudder at the approach of the giant, and he hid behind the coal scuttle. "Fee Fi Fo Fum," roared the giant. "I smell the blood of an Englishman. Be him live or be him dead, I'll break his bones to make my bread."

"Don't be silly," said the giantess, "you've never once changed your socks, and it's your feet you can smell."

Satisfied with this answer, the giant sat down and started to count his money. Jack sneaked a peek from his hiding place and saw a mountain of gold coins piled high on the table. Then the giant scooped it all back into the purse, put his feet on the table, and fell sound asleep.

When the thunderous snores convinced Jack that it was safe, he sneaked up on to the table. The purse was within reach, and Jack dragged it to the edge of the table where it fell with a tremendous KLUNK on to the floor. The giant slept on. Quickly Jack climbed down and dragged the purse to the castle door, and down to the meadow, and then down, down, down the beanstalk.

When Jack finally got back with his treasure he showed it to his mother who hugged him with joy, and warned him never to climb the beanstalk again.

But Jack decided that he would go back to the castle to find some more treasures, and when morning came again he got dressed and went down to the beanstalk to start the long climb all over again. Before he left the house, he tied a red scarf around his head, and painted freckles on his face, so that when he reached the top of the beanstalk and once again met the giantess, she would not recognise him.

Once again, she picked Jack up and popped him into her apron pocket, and warned him about the terrible giant. Once more, Jack hid as the castle trembled at the giant's approach.

"Fee Fi Fo Fum," roared the giant, "I smell the blood of an Englishman. Be him live or be him dead, I'll break his bones to make my bread."

"Tsk tsk," said the giantess, "the only thing you can smell is your armpits which have never been washed."

Satisfied with this answer, the giant sat down and called for his hen to be brought to him. Jack peeked around and saw to his amazement that the hen had laid a beautiful golden egg! Before long, the giant rested his head once more, then fell fast asleep.

When Jack heard the snoring, he sneaked up on to the table and gently took the hen, then quickly climbed down and carried it to the castle door, and down to the meadow and then down, down, down the beanstalk. When Jack returned once more with his treasure, his mother was waiting for him, and when Jack showed her the hen, she hugged him and begged him never to climb the beanstalk again.

But once again, Jack thought about the treasures in the castle, and the following morning he went down to the beanstalk to start the long climb all over again.

135

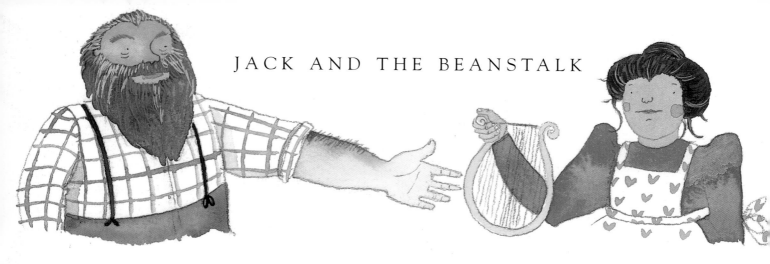

This time before he left the house, he tied a blue scarf around his head, and rubbed dirt into his face, and once again when he reached the top of the beanstalk and met the giantess, she did not recognise him. As before, she picked Jack up and popped him into her apron pocket, and warned him about the giant.

Again, the castle trembled at the approach of the giant. "Fee Fi Fo Fum. I smell the blood of an Englishman. Be him live or be him dead, I'll break his bones to make my bread," said the giant once again.

"What rot!" said the giantess. "That'll be all those bugs in your hair that's never been combed!"

Once more satisfied, the giant sat down and called for his harp to be brought to him. When the giant plucked at the strings of the harp, it magically started to sing in a clear soprano voice! The giant was soon lulled into a deep slumber across the table, and Jack wanted the beautiful harp so much that he didn't even wait for the snores! Jack climbed up to the table and put his hands on the harp to sneak it from under the nose of the sleeping giant, but to his horror, the harp started to shriek, "Help! Help! I'm being stolen."

136

The giant woke up. With a mighty roar he shouted, "Fee Fi Fo Fum, I smell the blood of an Englishman. Be him live or be him dead, I'll break his bones to make my bread." And with that he raced after Jack. But the giant wasn't as nimble as Jack, and Jack was able to rush out of the castle, down to the meadow and reach the top of the beanstalk with the giant in pursuit. Jack climbed down as quickly as possible, but the giant was not far behind him. The further down Jack climbed, the closer the giant got to him. When Jack was nearly at the bottom, he called to his mother to fetch the wood axe, and then Jack jumped the rest of the way to the ground. He grabbed at the axe and started to chop furiously at the stalk. The giant was almost down when the beanstalk crashed to the ground – right on top of him! The giant was squashed to nothing.

Now, with all the gold they had, Jack and his mother never needed to worry about money again.

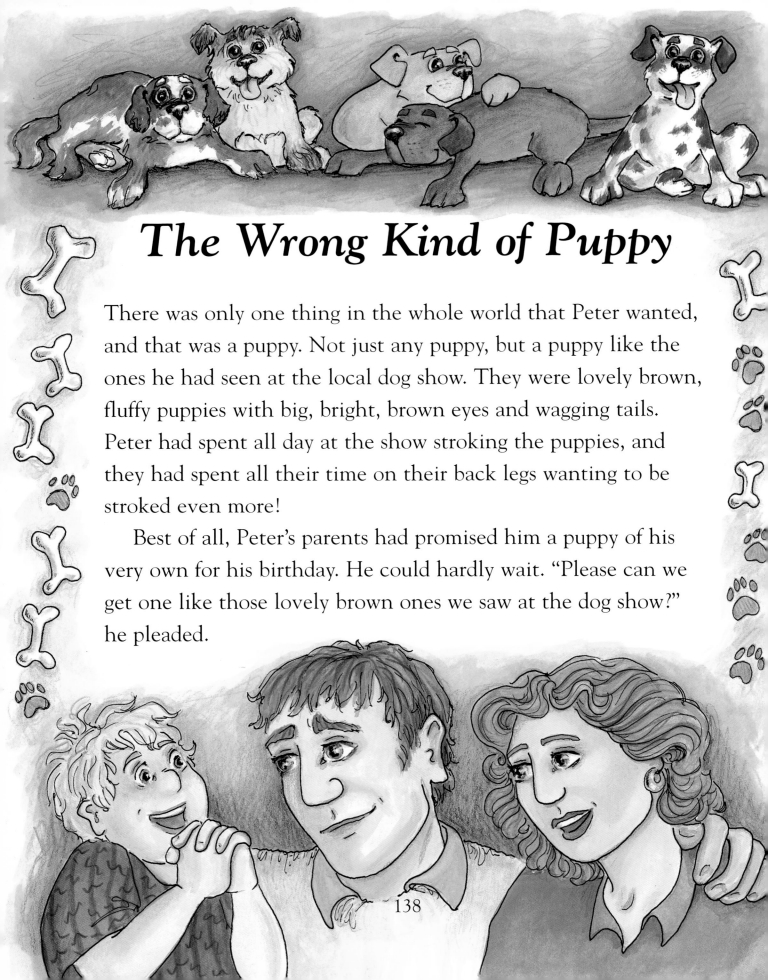

The Wrong Kind of Puppy

There was only one thing in the whole world that Peter wanted, and that was a puppy. Not just any puppy, but a puppy like the ones he had seen at the local dog show. They were lovely brown, fluffy puppies with big, bright, brown eyes and wagging tails. Peter had spent all day at the show stroking the puppies, and they had spent all their time on their back legs wanting to be stroked even more!

Best of all, Peter's parents had promised him a puppy of his very own for his birthday. He could hardly wait. "Please can we get one like those lovely brown ones we saw at the dog show?" he pleaded.

Peter's father shook his head and replied, "I'm sorry, son, but those were very expensive puppies, and they grow into very big dogs. We just couldn't afford one of those. But we will get you a puppy, I promise, and I'm sure you'll love it just as much."

Well, Peter was heartbroken. He had no idea that the puppies he had seen were expensive, but he just couldn't imagine loving any other sort of dog.

Eventually, Peter's birthday came around. In the morning, he woke up early to find a big pile of presents from his aunts, uncles and little sister. But where was his puppy? He was just about to burst into tears when he saw that one of the presents was from his parents. It was a big square box, but it certainly didn't feel like there was a puppy inside. He opened the box anyway, and discovered that it contained a collar, a lead, a dog bowl, a brush and comb and some bone-shaped biscuits. But still there was no puppy! Without opening any of his other presents, her ran into his parent's room (who were still asleep!) and asked where his puppy was.

"We have to go and collect it today," said his mother. "We've chosen you a lovely little puppy from the dogs' home that desperately needed a new family to look after it. We can go and get it as soon as we've had breakfast."

Peter was much too excited to eat any breakfast, of course, and spent the next half hour saying, "Can we go yet?" Eventually everyone was ready, and they all climbed into the car for the journey to the dogs' home. Peter sat in the back clutching the lead and hoping it wouldn't be too long before there was a puppy attached to the other end of it!

Soon they reached the dogs' home, and one of the kennel maids took them to where Peter's puppy was being kept. But when Peter first set eyes on the puppy, his heart sank. This wasn't anything like the sort of puppy he had wanted. Instead of being brown and fluffy and bouncy, this puppy was tiny and scraggy and timid. When it saw Peter and his family approach, it gave a little wag of its tail but then just stood in its cage whimpering

140

Now Peter had been taught by his parents that you must never be ungrateful for presents, even if they aren't exactly what you wanted. So although he was very disappointed, he reached out and stroked the puppy. The little scruffy puppy timidly approached Peter, licked his hand, and then ran off into the corner of the cage.

"He'll soon get used to you," said the kennel maid brightly. "Come on, Rags, time to go to your new home." And with that, she lifted the little puppy up and placed him in Peter's arms.

All the way home, the little puppy sat quietly in Peter's arms, occasionally trembling. Now and again he looked up at Peter with his big, soft eyes.

When they got Rags home, he was so frightened that he ran and hid under the curtains. Peter wondered how he was going to be able to play with such a timid friend.

Later that day Peter was sitting at the table having lunch when he felt something cold and wet against his leg; it was Rags's nose. He peered down to see Rags looking up at him, his tail wagging backwards and forwards. "He's looking a bit happier now," said Peter's father. "It will only be a matter of time before he feels really at home here."

The next morning, Peter hurried downstairs as soon as he awoke to say good morning to Rags – because the truth was, although Rags wasn't quite like the puppy he had expected, he was really getting very fond of him.

Rags jumped out of his basket when he saw Peter, his tail wagging furiously. "He's quite a waggy dog after all," thought Peter. Then Rags picked up his ball and began to play with it. Every time Peter tried to take it, Rags scurried off with a wag of his tail, looking round to make sure that Peter was chasing him. He seemed to like playing after all!

As the days went by, Rags seemed to grow more and more playful. He would jump up and greet his family with a big lick and a wagging tail, he always wanted to go for walks and to play, and he was very quick to learn tricks.

Peter just couldn't believe how much Rags had changed from the timid little creature in the dogs' home to the happy, playful puppy he was now – all thanks to a little love and care.

But the most curious thing of all was the puppy's appearance. He had now grown a beautiful, fluffy coat and, if Peter wasn't very much mistaken, it was quite brown, too. And it matched the colour of his big, brown eyes.

143

The Three Little Pigs

Once upon a time there were three little pigs who lived on a farm with their mother and father. They decided that, although they were just little pigs, they were quite grown up enough to make their way in the big wide world, so one day they set off together to make their fortunes.

After they had walked for quite some time, one of the little pigs started to feel rather tired. Just then, a farmer went by on his haycart.

"Hey, stop cart," the first little pig yelled. "You stronger brothers go on without me," he said. "This hay is light enough and soft enough for my house." And with that his brothers left the little pig with his pile of hay, and carried on their journey.

A little further down the road, the second little pig grew very tired. Just then, they passed by a forester cutting wood.

"Would you sell me some of your wood?" asked the second little pig. "This wood isn't too heavy and it isn't too rough for my house – it's just right." And with that the third little pig carried on his journey. Soon, even the third little pig grew very tired, and up ahead he spotted a builder making a wall out of stone.

"Aha," he thought, "that's exactly what I need to build my house, as it's strong and tough, just like me." And so he bought some stone and built himself a house.

That evening, just as the first little pig was settling comfortably in his bed of hay, he heard a rustling outside the house. He easily parted the hay with his hands to look outside, and gulped in fright when he saw the big bad wolf looking at him greedily.

"Little piggy, little piggy, will you let me in?"

"Not on the hairs of my chinny chin chin, I will not let you in," shuddered the first little pig.

"Then I'll huff, and I'll puff, and I'll blow your house down," said the big bad wolf.

And sure enough, he gave a little huff, and he gave a little puff, and with very little effort he blew the house down. Before the straw had settled to the ground, the little pig ran away as fast as his little legs would carry him to the home of his nearest brother.

The next evening, just as the two brothers were sitting down at their wooden table to eat their dinner, they heard scratching and sniffing outside the house. They peeked through the wooden window and gasped in alarm when they saw the big bad wolf staring at them hungrily. His stomach rumbled loudly.

"Little piggies, little piggies, will you let me in?"

"Not on the hairs of our chinny chin chins, we will not let you in," trembled the little pigs.

"Then I'll huff, and I'll puff, and I'll blow your house down," said the big bad wolf.

147

And sure enough, he huffed a bit, and he puffed a bit, and with a bit of effort he blew the house down. Before the planks of wood had crashed to the ground, the two pigs ran away as fast as their little legs would carry them to the home of their brother.

The next evening, just as the three brothers were making the fire to warm their toes, they heard crunching and crashing outside the house. The third little pig pulled a tiny stone out of the wall to make a peephole, and they all shrieked in terror when they saw the big bad wolf staring at them ravenously. His stomach grumbled even louder, and he was smacking his lips with glee at the feast waiting just a short breath away!

"Little piggies, little piggies, will you let me in?"

"Not on the hairs of our chinny chin chins, we will not let you in," quaked the three little pigs.

"Then I'll huff, and I'll puff, and I'll blow your house down," said the big bad wolf.

And sure enough, he took a big huff, and he took a big puff, and with a big effort he blew. But the house didn't blow down. So he took a bigger huff, and he took a bigger puff, and with the biggest of efforts he blew. But the house still didn't blow down. So he filled his lungs as full as he could and with a mighty effort he blew and blew and blew! And the house stayed up!

149

With that the big bad wolf started to climb up the stone wall to the chimney on the roof. The three little pigs looked around the stark stone room and then at each other in dismay – there was nowhere in here to hide, and nowhere left to run. They would have to stand and fight the big bad wolf!

Suddenly one of the little pigs had an idea, and whispered it into the ears of his brothers. They all ran over to the fireplace and hooked a huge pot of water over the roaring fire. They heard the wolf climb into the chimney. The water in the pot started to steam. They heard the wolf climbing down the chimney. The water started to bubble. They heard the wolf slide the rest of the way down the chimney and he landed splash in the middle of the pot of now boiling water. PLOP!

"AAARRRRHHHHH!" screamed the big bad wolf, leaping immediately out of the boiling pot. The three little pigs ran around the room trying to get away from the wolf, as the big bad wolf ran around the room trying to cool down, until eventually he ran straight through the stone wall, leaving a huge big bad wolf shaped hole, and carried on running and screaming and shouting all the way through the woods. That was the last they ever saw of the big bad wolf.

The three little pigs knew they had beaten the wolf, and he would never trouble them again, so they decided to build a brand new, comfortable house to live in. They built the walls of tough, strong stone. They made tables of smooth, warm wood, and they gathered lots of sweet-smelling, soft fresh hay to make comfortable beds. It was the best house in the world, and they all lived in it happily ever after.

Bobby's Best Birthday Present

It was the morning of Bobby's birthday and he was very excited. When he came down to breakfast, there on the table was a big pile of presents. Bobby opened them one by one. There was a beautiful book with pictures of wild animals, a toy racing car and a baseball cap. Bobby was very pleased with his presents, but where was the present from his parents? "Close your eyes and hold out your hands!" said his mother. When he opened his eyes there was a large rectangular parcel in his hands. Bobby tore off the wrapping and inside was a box. And inside the box was a wonderful, shiny, electric train set.

For a moment, Bobby looked at the train set lying in the box. It was so lovely he could hardly bear to touch it. There was an engine and six carriages all lying neatly on their sides. Bobby carefully lifted the engine out of the box. Then he set up the track and soon he had the train whizzing round his bedroom floor. Freddie the cat came in and watched the train going round. Round and round she watched it go, then one time when the train came past her she swiped at it with her paw and derailed it. The engine and the six carriages came tumbling off the track and landed in a heap on the floor. "Look what you've done!" wailed Bobby as he picked up the train and reassembled it. The carriages were undamaged, but the engine had hit the side of his bed and was badly dented.

Bobby was very upset. "My brand new train is ruined!" he cried.

"Don't worry, Bobby," said his mother, "we can't take it back to the shop now, but we can take it to the toymender in the morning. I'm sure he'll make a good job of mending the engine and it'll look as good as new again." Bobby played with his racing car, he wore his new baseball cap and he read his new book, but really all he wanted to do was to play with his train set. He went to bed that night with the engine on the floor near his bed.

In the morning when Bobby woke up, the first thing he did was to look at the poor broken engine of his train set. He picked it up, expecting to see the buckled metal, but the engine was perfect. He couldn't believe his eyes! He ran to his parents. "Look, look!" he cried. They were as amazed as he was. The engine worked perfectly and Bobby played happily with his train set all day – but he made sure Freddie kept out of his room!

That night Bobby couldn't sleep. He lay in bed tossing and turning. Then he heard a noise. It was the sound of his train set rushing round the track. He peered into the darkness and yes, he could definitely make out the shape of the train as it sped by. How had the train started? It couldn't start all by itself! Had Freddie crept into his room and flicked the switch? As his eyes gradually became accustomed to the dark Bobby could make out several shapes in the carriages. Who were the mysterious passengers? He slid out of bed and on to the floor beside the train set. Now he could see that the passengers were little folk wearing strange pointed hats and leafy costumes. "Elves!" thought Bobby.

At that moment one of the elves spotted Bobby. "Hello there!" he called as the train rushed past again. "We saw that your train set was broken. We so much wanted a ride that we fixed it. I hope you don't mind!" Bobby was too astounded to say anything at all. "Come with us for a ride," called the elf as his carriage approached again.

As the train passed him the elf leaned out of the carriage and grabbed Bobby by the hand. Bobby felt himself shrinking as he flew through the air, and the next instant he was sitting beside the elf in the carriage of his very own train set! "Here we go – hold tight!" called the elf as the train left the track and went out through the window into the night sky.

"Now, where would you like to go? What would you like to see?" asked the elf.

"Toyland!" replied Bobby without hesitation. Sure enough, the train headed towards a track which curved up a mountain made of pink and white sugar. Beside the track were toys going about their daily business. Bobby saw a ragdoll getting into a shiny tin car. Then a wooden sailor puppet wound up the car with a large key and off went the doll. He saw three teddy bears setting off for school with their satchels on their backs. Then he saw a brightly coloured clown playing a drum.

The train stopped and Bobby and the elves got out. "Now for some fun!" said one of the elves. They had come to a halt by a toy fairground. Bobby found that this was like no other fairground he had ever been to before. For in Toyland, all the rides are real. The horses on the carousel were real horses. The dodgem cars were real cars. And when he got in the rocket for the rocket ride, it took him all the way to the moon and back!

"Time to go, Bobby," said one of the elves at last. "It'll be morning soon." Bobby climbed wearily back into the train and soon he was fast asleep. When he woke up it was morning, and he was back in his bed. The train set lay quite still on its tracks. But in one of the carriages was a scrap of paper and on the paper, in tiny spidery writing, were the words: *We hope you enjoyed your trip to Toyland – the elves.*

The Wolf and the Seven Goats

There was once an old mother goat who had seven little goats. They all lived in a tiny house on the edge of a big, dark forest. One day, the mother goat had to go into the forest to collect food. Before she left, she called her seven little goats to her and said, "Now, children, promise me that while I am away you will lock the door and be on your guard against the wicked wolf. If you see him, don't let him in, because he would certainly eat you all up. You can recognize him by his gruff voice and his big black paws."

"Yes, mother," the little goats replied, "we promise to be very careful."

So the mother goat trotted cheerfully away into the forest, and the little goats locked the door. Some time later, there was a knock at the door, and the little goats heard a voice calling, "Open the door, children, it is your mother. I have brought back a present for each of you."

But the little goats heard that the voice was gruff, and not the gentle voice of their mother, and so they called, "No, we will not let you in! You do not have a soft voice like our mother's, you have a gruff voice. You are the wolf!"

159

So the cunning wolf went to a shop and stole a jar of syrup and swallowed it to make his voice soft. Then back he went to the little house by the forest. "Open the door, children," he called in his new, soft voice. "It is your mother. I have brought back a present for each of you."

Now the little goats heard the soft voice, but in his eagerness to get into the house the wolf had put his big black paws on to the window ledge, and so the little goats cried out, "No, we will not let you in! Our mother has beautiful white feet, but you have black feet. You are the wolf!"

So the wolf ran back into the village and went to the baker's shop, where he stole some flour and covered his paws in it. The wolf ran back to the little house by the forest. "Children, children, open the door!" he called again. "It is your mother. I have brought back a present for each of you."

The little goats heard the soft voice but they could not see any paws, and they called out, "Let us see your paws so that we know you really are our mother." So the wolf lifted up his paws, which of course were all white from the flour plastered on them. The little goats thought that this time it really was their mother, and they unlocked the door.

The wolf rushed in. The little goats screamed and tried to hide. One jumped into a drawer; the second squeezed under the bed; the third buried itself in the bedclothes; the fourth leaped into a cupboard; the fifth went into the oven; the sixth hid under a basin; and the littlest one slipped inside the grandfather clock. But the wolf found them and gobbled them up – all except the youngest one hiding in the grandfather clock.   When the wolf had finished his meal, he felt very full and very sleepy. He wandered out of the house into a nearby meadow, lay down on some dry leaves, and promptly fell asleep.

When the mother goat came home from the forest, imagine her horror as she saw the door open, the furniture strewn around the house and the little goats all gone. She started calling them by name, but nobody answered until she called out the name of the youngest little goat, who was still hiding in the grandfather clock. She quickly pulled him out, and then he told her what had happened to all his brothers and sisters.

She ran out of the house with the little goat trotting beside her and soon found the wolf sleeping in the meadow. She looked carefully at him and saw that there were six lumps in his fat stomach, and that they seemed to be moving. "My little goats are still alive," she exclaimed with joy.

Quickly she sent the youngest goat back to her house for scissors, needle and thread. Then, while the wolf was still sleeping, she carefully cut a hole in the wolf's stomach. Soon a little goat popped out and then another and another, until all six were free and jumping for joy. They had not come to any harm, for in his greed the wolf had swallowed them all whole.

"Quick," cried the mother goat, "fetch me some rocks from the river so that I can fill up this wicked wolf's stomach." So the little goats each fetched a rock and the mother goat sewed them up inside the wolf's stomach.

When the wolf awoke, he was very thirsty. "What is the matter with me?" he thought. "I shouldn't have eaten all those goats at once. Now I've got indigestion." He set out to drink from the river. But his stomach was so heavy he could hardly walk and he staggered to the water's edge. As he bent over to drink, the weight of the stones pulled the wolf into the water, where he sank straight to the bottom and drowned. Then the mother goat and all her little goats – who had been watching – danced for joy. For never again would they be afraid of the wicked wolf!

The Runaway Train

Once upon a time, there was a little kingdom in a far-off place. Although the people in the kingdom were ruled by a kindly king, the kingdom was mountainous and barren, and many of the folk were very poor.

Each month, there was a market. Market day was a very important day for all the villagers in the kingdom, just as it is for folk everywhere.

The market was held in a big, broad valley nestling among the snowy peaks, and people made their way to it from far and wide to sell their crops, or to buy new clothes or things for their home

People living up in the mountains would take the mountain passes and walk down into the valley. Those living a little further down the mountain would saddle up their donkeys and mules and ride to the market. But for people living at the bottom of the mountains, the best way to get to the market was to take the old steam train. The train ran from the bottom of the mountains all the way up to the top, and then down into the valley.

One day, a poor farmer who lived at the bottom of the mountains woke up and went to harvest the crops on his small farm. But the crop was poor. There was barely enough food to make a meal for his family and himself.

The poor farmer wondered what he could sell at the market, in order that his family and himself might have enough food to eat. He had no crops to sell, and he had already sold almost everything else he could spare. The only thing he had left to sell was his cockatoo.

The thought of selling his cockatoo filled him with great sadness. The cockatoo was a fine-looking bird, with colourful ivory, red and yellow feathers. Not only was it fine-looking, but it was thought by everyone to be a very clever bird, too. It seemed to understand whatever you said, and was a great favourite with all the family.

The farmer looked at his hungry family and then he looked at the cockatoo. The cockatoo looked back at the farmer as if it understood what the farmer was thinking.

"I must sell the cockatoo at the market," said the farmer finally. "We have no crops to eat, and we must buy food. There is nothing else we can sell to raise the money we need."

On the very next market day, the farmer climbed aboard the train for its journey up the mountains and down into the valley to the market. In his hand, he held a little metal cage, and sitting in the cage, looking very sad, was his beloved cockatoo.

The old train collected more people from the villages and then began its long, steep journey up the mountains. It chuffed and puffed, and puffed and chuffed, but then suddenly with a bang, a clang and a groan, it came to a halt. The boiler on the old train had exploded! Then, slowly, the train started to roll back down the mountain slope. The driver tried the brakes, but it was no use the old train just carried on rolling backwards, gathering speed all the time.

Everyone on board was very frightened, for there was nothing to stop the train hurtling all the way down the track and overturning at the bottom of the mountains.

Suddenly, the farmer had an idea. He lifted the cockatoo's cage close to his head and spoke to the cockatoo. "Fly down the mountain, as fast as you can, and raise the alarm!" he said. Then he opened the cockatoo's cage and released the bird.

Down the mountain the cockatoo flew as fast as its wings could take it. Straight to the railway station it went, and landed on the steps of the station master's office.

"Hello, what are you doing here?" said the station master, for he recognised the cockatoo by its bright, colourful feathers.

The cockatoo flew into the air and hovered in front of the station master, then it flew out of his office. Then it flew back into the office, flapped its wings in front of the station master and flew out again.

"Well, I do believe you want me to follow you," said the station master. So he went outside.

Suddenly something made the station master look up towards the mountain, and he saw the runaway train. "Quick!" he called to his station guards. "Bring some sand and follow me!" The station master and the guards quickly loaded sacks of sand. Then they threw it on to the track. Backwards and forwards they went with their sacks of sand, until a great mound of sand lay across the track, right in the path of the runaway train.

Suddenly the runaway train came into sight, clanking and rumbling helplessly down the track. Then it hit the heap of sand on the track and, amid more rumbling and grinding, it came to a safe halt.

Shaken, but safe, the passengers climbed out of the carriages. The station master explained what had happened and how the cockatoo had helped stop the runaway train.

"How could I ever have thought of selling you, my friend," said the farmer to his cockatoo. "From now on, we will always keep you safely."

All the villagers were so grateful to the farmer and his cockatoo, that they all gave some of their crops to help feed the farmer and his family until his own crops grew again.

Little Tim and His Brother Sam

Little Tim was a very lucky boy. He had a lovely home, with the nicest parents you could hope for. He had a big garden, with a swing and a football net in it. And growing in the garden were lots of trees that you could climb and have adventures in. Little Tim even had a nice school, which he enjoyed going to every day and where he had lots of friends. In fact, almost everything in Tim's life was nice. Everything that is apart from one thing – Tim's brother Sam.

Sam was a very naughty boy. Worse still, whenever he got into mischief – which he did almost all of the time – he managed to make it look as though someone else was to blame. And that someone was usually poor Tim!

Once Sam thought that he would put salt in the sugar bowl instead of sugar. That afternoon, Sam and Tim's parents had some friends round for tea. All the guests put salt in their cups of tea, of course, thinking it was sugar. Well, being very polite they didn't like to say anything, even though their cups of tea tasted very strange indeed! When Sam and Tim's parents tasted their tea, however, they guessed immediately that someone had been playing a trick. They had to apologise to their guests and make them all fresh cups of tea. And who got the blame? Little Tim did, because Sam had sprinkled salt on Tim's bedroom floor so that their mother would think that Tim was the culprit.

Another time, Sam and Tim were playing football in the garden when Sam accidentally kicked the ball against a window and broke it. Sam immediately ran away and hid, so that when their father came out to investigate, only Tim was to be seen. So poor little Tim got the blame again.

Then there was the time when Sam and Tim's Aunt Jessica came to stay. She was a very nice lady, but she hated anything creepy-crawly, and as far as she was concerned that included frogs. So what did Sam do? Why, he went down to the garden pond and got a big, green frog to put in Aunt Jessica's handbag. When Aunt Jessica opened her handbag to get her glasses out, there staring out of the bag at her were two froggy eyes.

"Croak!" said the frog.

"Eeek!" yelled Aunt Jessica and almost jumped out of her skin.

"I told Tim not to do it," said Sam.

Tim opened his mouth and was just about to protest his innocence when his mother said, "Tim, go to your room immediately and don't come out until you are told."

174

Poor Tim went to his room and had to stay there until after supper. Sam thought it was very funny.

The next day, Sam decided that he would play another prank and blame it on Tim. He went to the garden shed and, one by one, took out all the garden tools. When he thought no-one was watching, he hid them all in Tim's bedroom cupboard. In went the spade, the fork, the watering can, the trowel – in fact, everything except the lawnmower. And the only reason that the lawnmower didn't go in was because it was too heavy to carry!

But this time, Sam's little prank was about to come unstuck, for Aunt Jessica had seen him creeping up the stairs to Tim's bedroom with the garden tools. She guessed immediately what Sam was up to, and who was likely to get the blame. When Sam wasn't about, she spoke to Tim. The two of them whispered to each other for a few seconds and then smiled triumphantly.

Later that day, Sam and Tim's father went to the garden shed to do some gardening. Imagine his surprise when all he saw were some old flower pots and the lawnmower. He searched high and low for the garden tools. He looked behind the compost heap, under the garden steps, behind the sand pit and in the garage. But they weren't anywhere to be seen.

Then he started searching in the house. He looked in the kitchen cupboard, and was just looking under the stairs when something at the top of the stairs caught his eye. The handle from the garden spade was sticking out of the door to Sam's bedroom. Looking rather puzzled, he went upstairs and walked into Sam's bedroom. There, nestling neatly in the cupboard, were the rest of the tools.

176

"Sam, come up here immediately," called his father.

Sam, not realising anything was amiss, came sauntering upstairs. Suddenly he saw all the garden tools that he had so carefully hidden in Tim's cupboard now sitting in *his* cupboard. He was speechless.

"Right," said his father, "before you go out to play, you can take all the tools back down to the garden shed. Then you can cut the grass. Then you can dig over the flower beds, and then you can do the weeding."

Well, it took Sam hours to do all the gardening. Tim and Aunt Jessica watched from the window and clutched their sides with laughter. Sam never did find out how all the garden tools found their way into his bedroom, but I think you've guessed, haven't you?

No Hunting!

Mr Rabbit opened his eyes and gave a big yawn. He thought it seemed like the perfect day for going outside and nibbling some of the farmer's lettuces. And after that he thought he would go and see how well the farmer's carrots were growing, and maybe have a little nibble of those as well. He popped his head out of his burrow and looked this way and that, in case he saw any danger. Then he pricked up his ears and turned this way and that, in case he heard any danger. Finally, he sniffed the air this way and that, in case he smelled any danger. It seemed safe, so he hopped out of his burrow.

No sooner had he gone a couple of steps when "ZING" – a bullet whizzed past his head. Mr Rabbit jumped back into his burrow as fast as he could go, shaking with fright.

"Goodness, it's the rabbit hunting season," he gasped. He gathered his family of young rabbits around him and spoke to them. "Now children, listen very carefully," he said. "The rabbit hunting season has begun, so you must all stay safely inside the burrow until it's over. I will go out at night and forage for food for us all."

His children looked at him in dismay. "But it's lovely and sunny outside," they cried all together. "We'll be very careful."

But Mr Rabbit was having none of it. He insisted that they all stay under ground until the rabbit season was over.

For a few days, the young rabbits amused themselves as best they could by playing chase and hide and seek. But they were becoming very bored. Finally, they decided that they were going to do something to stop the rabbit hunting themselves.

First Tom, the eldest of Mr Rabbit's children, decided he would try and stop the hunters. So when it was dark, he crept out of the burrow and made his way towards the hunters' hut.

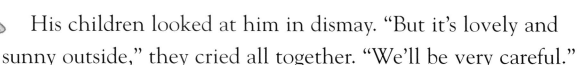

Although it was night and he was sure the hunters would be asleep, he was still very scared. Soon he came to the hut. It was standing in a clearing in the woods. It was dark inside the hut and he hoped the hunters were asleep. "If I can dig some big holes," he thought, "maybe they will fall into them in the morning and won't be able to get out until the hunting season is over."

So he dug and he dug like he had never dug before. Soon there were holes everywhere, right outside the door to the hunters' hut. Feeling very pleased with himself, but also very tired, Tom made his way back to the burrow just before it was light.

When the hunters awoke, they went straight out without falling down a single hole! Poor Tom, he had dug lots of holes alright, but the hunters' hut had two doors, and the hunters had simply gone out of the other one!

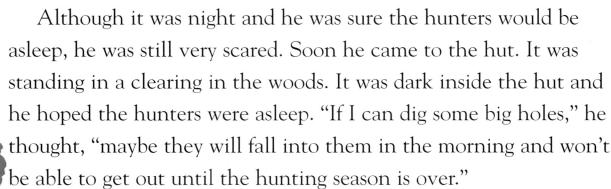

Then Jenny, the second oldest of Mr Rabbit's children, decided that she would try and stop the hunters. So when it was dark, she crept out of the burrow and made her way towards the hunters' hut. When she got there, she noticed that the window was open and so she decided to go inside. She, too, was very scared, but she thought about having to spend all those days in the burrow until the hunting season was over and that gave her the courage to carry on.

Inside the hut, she could see the hunters sleeping in their beds. She looked around, wondering what she could do to stop them hunting. Then suddenly she saw the hunters' clothes lying on a chair. Quick as a flash, she hopped up to them and started nibbling at them. In no time at all, the clothes were in shreds. "That'll stop them," thought Jenny. "They can't hunt without their clothes on!" Satisfied with her night's work, Jenny made her way back to the burrow just as dawn was breaking.

181

When the hunters awoke, they got straight up and went out hunting! Poor Jenny, she had chewed some clothes alright, but she had only chewed some spare clothes! The hunters had gone to bed wearing their other clothes in order to be out quickly in the morning.

Finally, Penelope, the youngest of Mr Rabbit's children, said she would try and stop the hunters.

"Don't be silly," said Tom to his sister. "You are far too young to be going out at night."

"And anyway," said Jenny, "what could you possibly think of doing to stop the hunters?"

"I'll think of something," said Penelope, who was really quite a clever little rabbit.

So that night, she crept out of the burrow and made her way to the hunters' hut. The window was open, just as before, and so Penelope hopped inside. She looked on the floor, she looked in the cupboards, and she looked under the beds, but she couldn't think of anything to stop the hunters.

Then she looked up and suddenly had an idea. For there on the table was a calendar, showing that very day's date. Penelope hopped on to the table and started to turn the pages. Finally she came to a page on the calendar that read: "RABBIT HUNTING SEASON ENDS TODAY". Satisfied with her work, Penelope hopped out of the hunters' hut and back home to her burrow.

In the morning, the hunters woke up, rubbed their eyes and got out of their beds. One of them glanced at the calendar. "Oh no!" he suddenly exclaimed. "Look at the date! The rabbit hunting season is over."

With that, the hunters (who were too silly to realise that someone else must have turned over the pages of the calendar) packed their belongings and went home. All was peace and quiet once more and the rabbits could hop about in the open air in safety.

Puss in Boots

Once upon a time in France, there lived a miller who had three sons. When he died, the miller left the mill to his eldest son. To his second son he left a donkey on whose back sacks of flour could be loaded and delivered to customers. But to the youngest son, who was much the most handsome of the three, he left only a large cat, whose job it had been to chase the mice that came at night to make holes in the sacks and steal grain.

The poor youngest brother wondered how on earth he would make his living with only the cat for company. He could see that he would have to go out into the world to seek his fortune. "I shall have to leave you behind, Puss," he said, "for I don't see how I am to look after you."

"What about if I looked after *you?*" replied Puss.

"Whatever do you mean?" said his master.

"I can make your fortune for you," said the cat. "All I need is a good – sized drawstring bag and a pair of really nice boots – for my hind feet."

Well, the lad was mightily puzzled, but he decided it was worth letting the cat try to win his fortune, as he surely had no idea of what to do otherwise. With his brand new boots on his hind paws and his drawstring bag slung over his shoulder, Puss set off with nothing but a handful of corn from the mill.

The first thing he did was go straight to the nearest rabbit warren where he opened the bag, put a little corn into it and laid it open near the rabbit hole. Then Puss laid in wait until dusk, when the rabbits came out of their hole. One rabbit came up, full of curiosity, and hopped into the bag to get the corn. Up sprang Puss and pulled the drawstring tight. Then, instead of taking the rabbit to his master, he set off to the palace, where he announced that he had brought the king a present.

"Your majesty," said Puss, taking a low bow, "I am a messenger from the Marquis of Carabas, your neighbour. He was out hunting today and was lucky enough to catch a fine young rabbit. He begs that you will accept it as a present."

The king was puzzled, because he'd never heard of this Marquis, but he was pleased to have the rabbit. "Tell your master that I am delighted with his kind present," he said.

Day after day, Puss went out hunting in this manner and each time he presented his catch to the king. "Don't forget," he said to his master, "that you're supposed to be a Marquis." The young boy had no idea what the cat was talking about, but he trusted him nevertheless. After a while the cat started to be invited in for a drink and a chat with the guards and he soon got to know all the court gossip. One time, Puss got to hear that the king was planning to drive the next day in his grand carriage with his daughter, the most beautiful princess in France. Puss took care to find out which direction they intended to take.

The next morning he said to his master, "I think it would be a good idea to take a swim in the river this morning." The lad agreed and, by the look in Puss's eye, he knew that he had a plan in mind. Puss led the way to a part of the river where the royal carriage was bound to pass. While the boy was swimming in the river, Puss heard the sound of the approaching carriage. Quickly Puss hid his master's ragged clothes under a stone and as the carriage came into view he ran into the road shouting, "Help! The Marquis of Carabas is drowning!" At once the king recognised Puss and ordered his guards to go to the rescue. The lad pretended to be drowning, so that the guards had quite a struggle to get him to the bank.

Meanwhile, Puss went up to the carriage, bowed to the king and said, "While he was bathing, thieves unfortunately stole my master's fine clothing. He cannot appear before your daughter without any clothes."

"Of course not," replied the king, and sent his footman to fetch a spare set of clothes from the back of the royal carriage. Now that the handsome lad was properly dressed, the king was glad to meet the mysterious Marquis, of whom he had heard so much from Puss. He welcomed the 'Marquis' into the carriage, where he sat next to the princess. "Come for a drive with us, my dear Marquis," said the king.

Without another word Puss set off and disappeared around the next bend of the road. By the time the king's gilded carriage was on its way again, Puss was a long way ahead. Soon he passed a field of haymakers. "My good haymakers," said Puss, "you must tell the king that this meadow belongs to the Marquis of Carabas – or I'll grind you all to little pieces."

Now Puss knew that the meadow really belonged to an ogre, who was known to be able to change his shape. So of course the haymakers had no idea if this was just an ordinary pussy cat telling them what to do – or if it really was the ogre. Soon the royal carriage passed by and the king leaned out and asked to whom the field belonged. "To the Marquis of Carabas, your majesty," chorused the haymakers.

"That's a fine piece of land you've got there," said the king, nudging the lad who was busy chatting to the princess.

All along the road it was the same story. Puss always got there before the royal carriage. Woodcutters, shepherds, and farmers all told the king that their master was the Marquis of Carabas, because Puss had threatened to turn them all into mincemeat if they didn't. Now Puss caught sight of a fine castle which he recognised as belonging to the ogre.

Puss went up to the great gate and asked to speak to the ogre. Puss said to him, "I heard that you can transform yourself in the most amazing way – into a lion for example. But I really can't believe that this is true."

The ogre was so offended that he bellowed, "JUST YOU WATCH!" and instantly turned himself into a lion. Puss pretended to be scared and jumped up on to the castle roof. The ogre turned himself back into an ogre. "That'll teach you," he roared.

"You gave me a dreadful fright," said Puss. "Do you know, people say you can even turn yourself into a tiny animal, such as rat or mouse. But that's absurd. It's quite impossible."

"IMPOSSIBLE, EH?" screeched the ogre, and the great foolish creature turned himself into a mouse.

In an instant, Puss had pounced on him and gobbled him up, bones and all. At that moment, the royal carriage rumbled over the drawbridge, for the king, too, had spotted the castle and wondered who lived there.

"Welcome to the castle of the Marquis of Carabas, your majesty," said Puss, who had just wiped the last morsels of the ogre from his whiskers.

"What," cried the king, turning to the young boy, "is this yours, too?" The lad glanced at Puss and then nodded. "May we see inside?" went on the king.

So the king, the princess and the miller's son looked around the castle. And very fine it was, too. The ogre's servants were so happy to see the back of their master that they laid on a fine feast. And at the end of the meal, the king agreed to give his daughter's hand in marriage to the 'Marquis'.

As for Puss, his master was so grateful that he saw to it that the cat was made a lord. So they all lived happily ever after and Puss never had to chase another mouse for the rest of his life.